"Sheriff...we've got another one."

The words sliced through Mac, and Callie grabbed his forearm as if to keep them both grounded. "Where?" Mac asked.

"It's Linda Bailey and she's in front of the bank," Cameron replied.

"We'll be there in five." Mac hung up and threw the car into Drive.

"Linda Bailey...she's another blonde," Callie said softly. In Mac's peripheral vision, he saw her reach up and touch one of her own blond curls.

Mac's stomach clenched tight and a faint nausea rose up inside him as he thought of Callie in the hands of this murderer. Still, right now all he should think about was that there was yet another innocent woman who had been killed.

What in the hell was happening? He was the sheriff in this town, and yet he felt as if he'd been dropped into the middle of a horror film where he didn't know the plot and couldn't see the end.

He was terrified for his town.

DEADLY DAYS
OF CHRISTMAS

———

New York Times Bestselling Author
CARLA CASSIDY

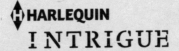

HARLEQUIN
INTRIGUE

HARLEQUIN®
INTRIGUE®

Recycling programs
for this product may
not exist in your area.

ISBN-13: 978-1-335-55544-1

Deadly Days of Christmas

This edition published by arrangement with Harlequin Books S.A.

For questions and comments about the quality of this book, please contact us at CustomerService@Harlequin.com.

Harlequin Enterprises ULC
22 Adelaide St. West, 40th Floor
Toronto, Ontario M5H 4E3, Canada
www.Harlequin.com

Printed in U.S.A.

Carla Cassidy is an award-winning, *New York Times* bestselling author who has written over 150 novels for Harlequin. In 1995, she won Best Silhouette Romance from *RT Book Reviews* for *Anything for Danny*. In 1998, she won a Career Achievement Award for Best Innovative Series from *RT Book Reviews*. Carla believes the only thing better than curling up with a good book to read is sitting down at the computer with a good story to write.

Books by Carla Cassidy

Harlequin Intrigue

Desperate Strangers
Desperate Intentions
Desperate Measures
Stalked in the Night
Stalker in the Shadows
Deadly Days of Christmas

Scene of the Crime

Scene of the Crime: Bridgewater, Texas
Scene of the Crime: Bachelor Moon
Scene of the Crime: Widow Creek
Scene of the Crime: Mystic Lake
Scene of the Crime: Black Creek
Scene of the Crime: Deadman's Bluff
Scene of the Crime: Return to Bachelor Moon
Scene of the Crime: Return to Mystic Lake
Scene of the Crime: Baton Rouge
Scene of the Crime: Killer Cove
Scene of the Crime: Who Killed Shelly Sinclair?
Scene of the Crime: Means and Motive

Visit the Author Profile page at Harlequin.com.

CAST OF CHARACTERS

Callie Stevens—Dispatcher turned deputy to catch a serial killer. She also has a major crush on the sheriff.

Mac McKnight—Sheriff of the small town of Rock Ridge, Kansas. He's tested to his limits by a serial killer terrorizing his town.

Roger Lathrop—A smooth-talking insurance salesman who had a volatile history with two of the victims.

Nathan Brighton—The town's handyman. He was seen in the area of two of the murders. Is it possible he's the killer?

Ben Kincaid—He sees evil spirits. Is it possible he saw the young women as evil and killed them?

Chapter One

Callie Stevens walked briskly down the sidewalk toward the sheriff's department in the distance. December 1 began her most favorite time of the year—the coming of the holidays.

Overnight the street crews of Rock Ridge, Kansas, had worked to hang red-and-white lights in the shapes of candy canes on each streetlamp, along with greenery that added to the festive aura.

She loved Christmas and this year she was determined to bring a little bit of the holiday into her work space, something that had been an unspoken taboo for the past two years she'd worked as a receptionist-dispatcher for Sheriff Mac McKnight.

Her cheeks warmed a little against the unusually cold, blustery air as she thought of Sheriff Hottie, her secret nickname for him. If this year went as the last year had, Sheriff Hottie's cranky mood would begin today and last through the holidays.

"We need a little Christmas," she murmured beneath her breath and then opened the back door of the sheriff's office. Her shift was four in the afternoon to midnight, when Glenda Rivers came in to relieve her. She went into the break room, where Johnny Matthews greeted her with a wide smile. "Cold out there, right?"

"Too cold for so early in the season," she agreed as she hung up her white winter coat on one of the hooks protruding from the wall on one side of the room. "Anything popping this evening?" she asked.

"Absolutely nothing," Johnny replied. He took a swig of his soda and then set the can back on the table. "I think it's going to be a long, boring night. It's too cold for even the crazies to be out."

She laughed. "Don't sound so depressed, Johnny. That's the way we're supposed to want things…boring. Who else is on tonight?"

"Cameron and Adam. They're out on patrol right now." Johnny downed the last of his soda, crushed the can and then stood. He was a good-looking guy with dark hair and brown bedroom eyes.

He'd made it clear on more than one occasion that he wouldn't mind going out with her, but Callie had no interest in dating him. She thought of him more like a big brother. She just felt no chemistry with him.

"Guess I'll hit the road," he said and grabbed his coat off one of the hooks. "You still haven't bought a car?"

"No." Callie released a deep sigh. Her old car had finally died two months ago with the repair estimate being more than the car's worth. "Every time I think about the whole process of getting a new one, I get a headache. I can walk to work and to pretty much all the stores on Main Street. I keep asking myself why I really need a car."

"On days like this when the cold wind blows, it's nice to have a car to take you where you need to go," Johnny replied and then laughed. "I think I almost made a rhyme. Now I'd better get back to work."

"Stay safe out there," Callie said.

"Always," Johnny replied. As he went out the back door, Callie left the break room and headed up the hallway toward the reception area.

She passed Sheriff McKnight's office door. It was closed but she knew he was probably in there. He was almost always here or out on the streets. It wasn't unheard-of for him to still be here in the office at midnight and be back at seven in the morning. The man was definitely a workaholic.

"Hey, Callie," Maggie Jones greeted her and rose from the desk. "I have a feeling it's going to be a long, boring shift for you. The phone hasn't rung all day."

Maggie was the grandmother of ten, but she refused to be one of those grannies who sat home and baked cookies. With her brassy red hair and raucous laughter, she had been a fixture in the sheriff's office for years.

"I always bring a book with me in case things are really slow," Callie replied. "And today I also brought this…" She reached into her purse and withdrew the large red-and-white candle and set it on the desk. "This will make the whole place smell like peppermint."

"Oh girl, you know that's not a good idea," Maggie replied and cast a quick glance down the hallway.

"Surely he can't complain about one simple little candle," Callie protested.

"A candle that smells like Christmas," Maggie said, raising one of her red eyebrows. "I love Mac to death, but you know he's like Scrooge around this time of the year."

"I'm sure it will be fine," Callie said with a touch of false bravado.

Maggie got up from the desk and laughed. "I just hope you're alive for your shift tomorrow." Maggie gathered up her things and with a goodbye she headed out the front door.

Callie placed the candle on the desk, her purse on the floor, and then sank down in the desk chair. In a small town like Rock Ridge there was nothing technical or complicated about being a dispatcher. Her job was to answer the phone, facilitate help for anyone who came through the doors and use her radio to stay in touch with the officers on duty.

Most of the calls that came in were non-emergency issues, so her job was relatively undemanding. What she really wanted was to become a deputy and work side-by-side with the sheriff.

After high school she had moved to Kansas City and had gotten her degree in criminal justice. She'd landed a job as a deputy on a small-town force just outside the city and life had looked bright. Then tragedy had struck.

She shook her head, unwilling to allow any sad thoughts to intrude into her head at the moment. She got out a lighter from her purse and lit the candle and then settled in for work.

Everything remained quiet for the next hour or so and then she heard the ominous creak of Mac's office door opening. She glanced at the flickering candlelight as his footsteps came closer and then she drew in a deep breath for courage.

As always, her heart fluttered a bit in anticipation of seeing him. There was just something about Mac that made her feel like a breathless teenage girl with a crush.

He stepped into the reception area. He was a tall, broad-shouldered man. His dark hair was cut short and his features were well-defined. Lordy, the man was hot. His gray eyes now shot to the candle and then back to her.

"Afternoon, Callie," he said, his low, deep voice shooting warmth right to the center of her belly.

"Afternoon, Sheriff," she replied.

Once again his gaze shot to the candle throwing out the sweet scent of peppermint. She heard him draw in a deep breath. "I'm heading to the café for an early dinner," he said. "If you need anything in the next hour or so, that's where I'll be."

"Enjoy," she replied, happy that he said nothing about the candle.

As he headed out the front door, she couldn't help but admire how his khaki pants fit over his sexy butt and down his long legs. She released a deep sigh as he disappeared from her sight.

She'd been working here for almost two years and on most days, she wasn't even sure Mac noticed her at all. He obviously had no idea that she was crazy mad in love with him.

All she wanted was for him to really *see* her, to allow her to bring a little joy into his life. Because she had a feeling from everything she'd seen of the man, he appeared to have little or no joy in his life. To Callie, there was just something a little bit sad about him.

Of course, if he knew she thought that about him, he'd probably be highly offended. He was a strong and proud man who loved his town and had committed his entire career to keeping the citizens safe. The deputies who worked with him all adored him and considered him a fair and supportive employer.

She was twenty-seven years old and wanted to be with the man of her dreams. She wanted to be loved and cared about and begin planning a family. It was unfortunate that the man of her dreams didn't know she was anything other than a capable dispatcher.

The ring of the phone pulled her from her thoughts of Mac. She took the call and then an hour later Mac walked back into the office. As always, her heart quickened in pace just a little bit.

"How was your dinner?" she asked.

"It's always good at the café," he replied. "I had the Tuesday-night special."

"Meatloaf with mashed potatoes and corn," she said with a grin.

"You must eat there often to know the daily specials."

"On my nights off I usually grab dinner at the café," she replied.

"Anything happen while I was gone?"

"Daisy Miller called."

A slow, lazy grin curved his mouth, half-melting Callie's heart. "Let me guess. Bubba got out again and she wanted all the deputies to come over and get him back into the house."

"You got it." Bubba was Daisy's miniature pet pig and about once a week the pig somehow got out of the house and into Daisy's yard. "I told her somebody would get back to her and fifteen minutes later she called again to say she'd coaxed Bubba back into the house with a pan full of roast beef and vegetables."

"I wouldn't believe it was a normal week if Daisy didn't call about Bubba," he replied. "And now I'm going to head out on patrol for a couple of hours."

With a murmured goodbye, he headed down the hallway and exited out the back door and Callie settled back in for another long, boring night.

Mac was back at eight and returned to his office. The deputies came and went, talking and teasing with her and breaking up the monotony of her job.

At ten until midnight Glenda Rivers showed up to relieve Callie. Glenda had just greeted Callie when the phone rang. Callie picked up. "Rock Ridge Sheriff's Department," she said.

"I just murdered a woman. Her body is on Main Street," a deep voice said.

Callie frowned. Was this some kind of a joke? "May I ask who is calling?" The caller identification showed an anonymous number.

"That doesn't matter. She's on a bench in front of the post office." Whoever it was then hung up.

Callie immediately jumped up from the desk, so disturbed by what she'd just heard that she didn't think about calling Mac on the radio. Instead, she raced down the hallway and burst into his office.

"Mac… Sheriff, I just got a call that there's a body of a murdered woman on Main Street on the bench in front of the post office," she explained.

Mac rose from his desk. "Who called it in?"

"It was an anonymous call," she replied. "It was a male, but I didn't recognize the voice." She watched as he pulled on his winter coat. "Mac, could I ride along with you? Glenda is here to take over the desk. Please, you know I've been asking forever to shadow you for more experience."

He hesitated a moment and frowned. "Okay, grab your coat and meet me at my car."

Callie didn't waste any time. She went up front and grabbed her purse, then raced down the hallway and into the break room to grab her coat. This was what she'd been waiting for. She'd wanted an opportunity to work with him. At least now maybe he would be able to see that she'd make a good deputy…or better yet that she'd make a great girlfriend.

"COLDEST NIGHT OF the year and somebody has put a body on a bench? It's got to be a hoax," Mac said as he started his patrol car. "There hasn't been a murder around here in the past four years and that one was a domestic that went bad."

"That was obviously before my time here," Callie replied.

"Yeah, it was," he agreed. He tore out of the parking lot behind the office and turned onto Main Street. He cast a quick glance at her.

With her curly blond hair, sparkling blue eyes and ready smile, she looked more like a cheerleader than a wanna-be deputy. She smelled like crisp fresh flowers with a hint of cinnamon and vanilla. She also smelled of danger...the kind of danger that could get a man into trouble.

He wasn't even sure why he'd allowed her to come with him other than the fact that she asked frequently to ride with him and in the chaos of the strange phone call he'd had a weak moment.

He found her attractive and sexy as hell, so he tried to keep his distance from her. He had no desire to have a relationship of any kind with any woman. He preferred being alone.

He emptied his head as he drew closer to the post office. At least it was cold enough and late enough that the streets and sidewalks were empty of people.

And then he saw her. Despite what had been done to her he immediately recognized her. The dead woman on the bench was Melinda Tyson, a waitress at the café.

"Oh my God," Callie said with a gasp.

Mac pulled his car to a stop. "Stay here," he said to Callie and then he jumped out and hurried to Melinda. She was a horrifying sight, posed with a little red Santa hat on her blond hair and with a dead bird in her mouth. What the hell?

If she still had a pulse, if she had any sign that she still clung to life, he'd do what he could to sustain that life until an ambulance from the hospital could come.

As he got closer to her, he knew she was dead, but he still checked her wrist for a pulse. Nothing. Her eyes were wide open and already had the pale cast of death in them. There was nothing he could do to help her at this point.

He returned to the car and got on his radio, calling all available deputies to the site. He then called undertaker–medical examiner Richard Albertson.

"I've got some protective gear in the trunk," he said to Callie. "We should at least put on some booties and gloves until the scene has been thoroughly processed."

He gazed at her for a long moment. "It's a fairly gruesome scene. Are you okay?"

"If you're expecting me to throw up or dissolve into hysterics, you'll be disappointed because I'm just fine," she replied. "I'm horrified, but I'm good." She raised her chin as if to prove to him she was okay.

"Then let's get moving."

Minutes later they both wore plastic booties and gloves and by that time Deputies Johnny Matthews and Cameron Royal and two more deputies had joined them.

Cameron began photographing the scene, Johnny and the other two deputies collected any and all potential evidence around the bench and Mac wrote down his impressions about the body while Callie stayed back to observe.

Melinda had been stabbed at least five times that he could see, although there was no blood around the bench, letting Mac know she had been killed elsewhere.

She was clad in black slacks and a light blue sweatshirt. There was no coat or purse anywhere around her to be found.

The Santa hat might just be a nod to the upcoming holiday. However, it was the bird in her mouth that was horrifying and made no sense. It was a bobtail quail, fairly common in their county. Mac knew making sense of it would be imperative in solving the murder. Was the fact that it was specifically a quail important or would any bird have done?

Richard Albertson arrived on scene with his assistant, Dean Cooper. Mac stepped back next to Callie as the medical examiner did his preliminary exam.

Mac had only worked with the tall, thin man on a murder case once in Mac's seven years as sheriff. That had been an open-and-shut case where the guilty party was on scene and confessed to hitting his wife with a baseball bat and killing her in a fit of rage.

Melinda, with a dead bird shoved in her mouth and a Santa hat on her head, was a whole different animal. This was the kind of case that would give law enforcement officials dark and horrible nightmares until the killer was caught.

It took almost an hour for Albertson to finish his exam. "There are ligature marks around her wrists and ankles," he began. "My initial guess would be some kind of a rope, but I'll know more about that after getting her on my table."

"Time of death?" Mac asked.

Richard frowned. "Time of death is a bit of an issue with the temperature and not knowing exactly how long she's been out here in the elements," he said to Mac. "But, due to the fact that rigor mortis hasn't set in yet, my guess is she's been dead no longer than about two hours."

"Cause of death?" Mac asked, although it didn't take a rocket scientist to know she'd been stabbed to death.

"My initial finding is death by stabbing, but again I won't know for sure until I get her on the autopsy table. Right now my ruling is death by homicide." His round brown eyes appeared owlish in the headlights from Mac's vehicle. "If you're finished gathering evidence, then Dean and I are ready to transport the body to my office. If you want to stop by my office within the next couple of hours, I'll try to have a better workup for you."

"Sounds good," Mac replied.

It was just after two when the body was finally carried away and all the potential evidence had been collected. Mac and Callie got back into his car.

"Now I have to do one of the most difficult things my job entails," he said with a deep sigh. Mac had kept his emotions turned off from the moment he'd seen the body until now. But now, along with the sadness of the loss of a life, a rage built up inside him. He was determined to find the person who had done this to a young woman in the town he loved.

"What's that?" Callie asked.

"Make notification to Melinda's parents. I don't want to wait and risk the chance they'll hear it from anyone before they hear it from me."

"We were lucky there was nobody else to see her except law enforcement officials," she said.

He nodded. "I'll go ahead and take you home before I go to their place."

"That isn't necessary. Maybe I can help... You know, a woman's touch and all that."

A woman's touch. God, it had been a long time since he'd felt a woman's touch. And now he found himself wondering what it would feel like to have Callie running her slender hands across his body.

Dammit. He shook his head to empty it of any inappropriate thoughts. Apparently, it was easier to think of the woman seated next to him than the murder he needed to solve.

When he pulled up in front of the Tysons' home a hard knot of tension formed in his gut. He knew Connie and Eddie Tyson. They were good people who had always supported him and he knew how much they loved their daughter.

He cut his engine and stared at the darkened house. He was about to wake up the couple, tear their lives apart and rip a hole in their hearts that would always be there.

"Let's get this over with," he finally said and together he and Callie got out of the car and headed to the front door. An hour later they returned to the car.

Mac had left out the gory details of Melinda's death, but telling parents their beautiful daughter had been stabbed to death had been difficult enough.

He'd actually been grateful Callie had been with him. As Connie fell to the sofa and began to sob, it had been Callie who had held her while Eddie had expressed his grief by yelling and swearing that once the perpetrator was found he was going to kill him.

By the time Mac and Callie left their home, Connie and Eddie were on the sofa together, sitting in the kind of silence that positively screamed with pain and grief too enormous to express.

Callie was silent on the ride home and Mac appreciated the quiet. It was almost three in the morning, far too late tonight to speak to people about Melinda. He'd asked her parents a few questions and had learned that Melinda wasn't dating anyone at the moment, and that lately she'd mostly hung out with people from the café where she worked.

Melinda usually walked to and from work, unless she caught a ride with one of her friends. When she'd left the house that morning she'd been wearing a red-and-blue winter coat. She had worked an early shift at the café and when she hadn't come home from that shift, her parents had just assumed she'd gone out with friends. As an adult living at home with her parents, she had no curfew and her parents often didn't know what her plans were for any particular day.

This heinous murder was the kind that would haunt those who had seen Melinda with that bird stuffed in her mouth. It was definitely the stuff of nightmares.

Tomorrow he'd have a full plate interviewing coworkers and friends of Melinda. At the moment, a tension headache stretched and tightened painfully across his neck. He rubbed it in an effort to ease the pain.

Once again, he could smell Callie's evocative perfume, but this time he welcomed the fragrance after the scents of death and grief that filled his head.

He knew she usually walked to work, but

there was no way in hell he was going to allow her to walk home from the sheriff's office at this time of night with the wind chill hovering around freezing and a murderer on the loose.

"Mac." Callie finally broke the silence as he pulled in front of the attractive two-story house where Callie lived on Main Street. He cut the engine and then turned to look at her.

She looked so pretty in the illumination from the dashboard. Had her eyelashes always been that long? Had her hair always looked so shiny and touchable?

"I want to help you with this investigation," she said. "Couldn't you deputize me just for this case and let me be an active participant in catching this creep? You know you can call in Dana Jeffries to take over my shift as dispatcher. She's always eager to work."

The words tumbled out of her mouth fast and furiously. "You only have a small force of deputies and you could use one more working on this case. I have all the qualifications to be a deputy and I really think I could be a big help. Please, Mac. Let me be a part of this."

She looked so intense…so earnest and there was no question he had a feeling he could definitely use another deputy working on this case. Still, he hesitated. Would she be a help or a distraction to him?

"I'll think about it," he finally said.

"You can't give me an answer now?" she asked.

"I said I'll think about it," he repeated in a tone that didn't invite further conversation on the matter.

"Okay, then I'll see you tomorrow." She opened the car door. "Good night, Mac."

"Good night, Callie." He watched as she walked to the front door and then disappeared into the house.

He pulled away from the curb and headed toward the Albertson's Funeral Home. Despite the lateness of the hour, he hoped the medical examiner would have worked up a preliminary report by now.

This was the first time Mac would be challenged as a sheriff, as a man who wanted to keep the people in his town safe. He'd been found inadequate before in his life and that inadequacy had not only destroyed his love of Christmas, but also his ability to ever open his heart again.

He didn't care about the holiday or ever loving again. What he cared about right now was finding the person who had killed Melinda. He definitely hoped this was a one-and-done kind of murder.

However, as he pulled up in the back of the funeral home, he had a very bad feeling about this.

Chapter Two

Mac sank down at his desk a few minutes after seven. He hadn't gone to bed the night before until just before four. He now had before him the initial autopsy report that Richard Albertson had provided to him this morning. Unfortunately, he hadn't had it ready the night before when Mac had stopped by.

Thankfully, he didn't believe anyone in town other than his team had seen Melinda's body. He intended to keep the bird in her mouth and the Santa hat on her head from the public.

He continued to read the report, and was nearly through it when there was a knock on his door. "Come in," he called.

He raised an eyebrow in surprise as Callie walked in. "Good morning," she said with a bright smile. She was clad in a pair of jeans that hugged her long, slender legs and a royal blue blouse that did amazing things to her eyes. The scent of her eddied in the air, a scent he'd noticed the day before and found incredibly attractive.

She carried with her a handful of papers and a foam cup of coffee from his favorite coffee shop. "This is for you," she said and placed the cup on his desk in front of him. "It's made just the way you like it with a teaspoon of sugar and a dollop of cream."

He stared at the cup and then looked back at her. "Is this meant to be some sort of a bribe to get the deputy job?"

Her eyes widened and a charming pink danced into her cheeks. "Oh... I didn't think about it that way." She appeared truly shocked by the very idea. "I... I just figured you were probably up really late last night and I've seen you carry in a cup of coffee from the Beanery before and I just thought..." Her voice trailed off.

"It's fine, Callie," he said with a smile. "I appreciate your thoughtfulness. And for future purposes, if you are going to try to bribe me, I'd expect a muffin or a cinnamon roll to go with the coffee."

She smiled. "Duly noted." She slid into the chair facing him. "I did a little research when I got home last night into the bobtail quail."

He looked at her in surprise. He knew what time she had gotten home the night before. The fact that she had done anything but go straight to sleep was definitely admirable.

"What did you find out?" he asked, certainly interested in any information she might have about the bird that had been stuffed in Melinda's mouth.

He was aware of time ticking away. He had two of his deputies already out talking to people around town to see if anyone had been on the streets the night before around the time that Melinda's body had been left. Mac wanted to get to the café and start talking to people there sooner rather than later. But the bird might be the key to finding the murderer.

She looked down at her papers. "I could give you all the yada yada about species and subspecies, but I don't think any of that is really important in this case. What I do think might be important is that the whistle they make sounds like 'bob-WHITE,' so maybe it's possible our murderer's name is a derivative of that. The species was once considered to be monogamous, but their behavior is now described as ambisexual polygamy."

She glanced up at him. "Am I boring you or do you want me to go on?"

"Absolutely go on," he replied. He'd never noticed before what a pleasant voice she had; it was low and more than a little bit sexy. More importantly, she was telling him things about the bird that might be vital to this case.

She returned her gaze to her papers. "Really, the only other thing is that the birds are shy and elusive and rely on camouflage to stay undetected." When she looked back up at him a tiny wrinkle danced across her forehead. "So, it's possible our perp somehow identifies with the bobwhite. Maybe his name is White or some derivative and it might be possible he's shy and reclusive."

"Maybe. Thanks for your research into this. You've definitely saved me some time." He knew her shift on the dispatcher desk officially began at four, but here she was at seven in the morning giving him information that might be important to the murder.

He studied her for several long moments. She'd shown initiative and he liked that. Her eyes also shone with a fierce determination, an eagerness to be a part of the investigation.

He opened his desk drawer and pulled out a deputy badge, a police-issued revolver and a holster. He set the items on the desk and pushed them toward her. Her eyes widened once again and then joy filled her features.

God, he couldn't remember the last time he'd felt anything remotely close to joy.

"Really?" she said, her voice half-breathless.

"Go on, take them," he said. "Get a uniform from the supply closet and get into it. You are a deputy until four o'clock today and then we'll see how things are going. You haven't officially been sworn in, so you'll ride with me and only do what I tell you to. Now, meet me at my car in about fifteen minutes. We've got a full day ahead of us."

She picked up the badge and clasped it to her heart, then grabbed the holster and revolver and jumped out of the chair. "I swear you won't be sorry about this," she said and then practically raced out the door.

He picked up the phone, made a quick call and then grabbed his coat and headed down the hallway. As he passed the break room he glanced inside. Nobody was there, but there was a stuffed Santa sitting on top of the soda machine.

He knew it was Callie's doing. Nobody else would have the nerve to bring in anything remotely to do with Christmas. All his staff knew how he felt about the holiday.

Still, he had more important things to think about besides a stuffed doll. He headed out the door and to his car, where Callie stood by the passenger door, her coat in her hand. He'd never thought of their uniforms as being sexy, but on Callie the khaki outfit appeared to be made just for her.

The shirt fit her frame perfectly, showcasing her slender waist and the thrust of her breasts. The slacks hugged her long legs and a rivulet of warmth swept through him despite the cold temperature.

He frowned as he unlocked the car. She threw her coat into the back seat and then the two of them got inside. Maybe it was a bad idea for him to have her with him. However, there was no way he intended to let her loose to do her own thing. She was far too green to be out on her own and he hadn't really sworn her in properly.

"I just finished reading the autopsy report," he said once they were both in the car. He'd rather stay focused on the murder than anything he might feel toward his sexy new deputy.

"And?"

He could feel her curious gaze on him as he backed out of his parking space. "We will have to wait on some lab results, but she was stabbed twenty-three times."

"Wow, definitely overkill indicating rage," she replied.

A pleasant surprise filled him at her response. It was exactly what he believed. He just hadn't expected her to pick up on it.

"So, knowing that, what would be the next thing you'd believe?" he asked.

"That the murder was personal, probably committed by somebody close to her."

"That's what I'm thinking, so we're headed to the café to talk to the people she worked with to see what we can discover," he said.

"Sounds like a plan," she agreed.

He doubted that anyone at the café, except the murderer, knew about the murder. Other than the notification to Melinda's parents in the middle of the night, nobody else in town should know.

"What about her missing coat and purse? Do you think the murderer kept them as trophies?" she asked.

"Hard to tell at this point, but I had several of my men check Dumpsters last night looking for the items and they didn't find them," he replied.

"And the ligature marks?" she asked.

"Albertson was ninety percent certain they were made by ropes. Whatever happened to her, it appears she was tied with her wrists and ankles to something."

"It's so tragic," she said softly.

"I definitely agree," he said.

He had to park down the block from the café, as all the parking spaces in front were taken. Seven days a week half the town folks could be found having their first meal of the day in the café. It was the place where gossip ran rampant, the food was great and the coffee was always fresh and hot.

The first person he wanted to talk to was Jimmy Jo Jacobs, aka JJ, the owner and head cook in the café. He and Callie walked in together. The scents of frying bacon and onions and fresh baked goods filled the air, along with the sounds of clinking silverware and the chatter of all the diners.

Linda Richards, one of the waitresses and acting hostess, greeted them. "You two need a table or a booth?" she asked.

"Neither. We aren't here to eat. We need to speak with Jimmy," Mac said.

She waved toward the doorway that led into the kitchen. "He's back there."

With a nod, Mac and Callie headed to the kitchen area. Jimmy Jo was a big man, a walking advertisement for his excellent home-cooked food. When they entered the back, he was working the grill and barking orders to two other cooks.

"Jimmy," Mac yelled to be heard above the din.

The bald man turned to look at Mac in surprise. "Sheriff, what can I do for you? Eggs too runny? Toast burned?"

"No, nothing like that, but we need to talk to you…privately," Mac replied.

Jimmy laid down the wide metal pancake turner he'd been using to flip frying bacon. He wiped his hands on the white apron that stretched across his big belly. "Chris, take over here," he said to one of the men. "Let's go on back to my office," he said to Mac and Callie.

They followed Jimmy through the kitchen and to a small room in the back. Besides holding a variety of supplies, there was also a small desk with a couple of folding chairs in front of it.

"What's up?" Jimmy asked once they were all seated.

"Melinda Tyson was murdered last night," Mac said.

"Oh my God." Jimmy sat back in his chair, obviously shocked. "I wondered why she didn't show up for work this morning."

"Did she work yesterday?" Mac asked.

"She did. She worked the early-morning shift and got off work at eleven." Jimmy shook his head. "She's really dead? I can't believe it. She was a good kid and a hard worker."

"Did she mention where she might be going after she got off work yesterday?" Callie asked.

Jimmy shook his head. "Not to me, but she might have mentioned something to Shelly Steward. She and Melinda were pretty tight as friends. You want me to call Shelly in to talk to you?"

"That would be great," Mac replied.

"Hopefully Shelly will be able to fill in some blanks as to what Melinda did after work yesterday," Callie said once Jimmy had left the office.

Mac nodded. It was definitely important to trace a victim's movements in the hours prior to their death. Somebody somewhere might have seen something that could blow the lid right off the case.

The word would be out now. He figured within hours everyone would know about the murder and all the people in town would be looking to him for answers.

As a member of the law enforcement team, Callie would also now be under scrutiny. Was she really up to the pressure…the stress that was about to take over her life? More importantly…was he?

CALLIE SAT QUIETLY and watched as Mac questioned Shelly. Initially when the auburn-haired Shelly had learned why they were speaking with her, she had burst into tears at the news her friend had been murdered.

Callie admired Mac's gentleness with the grieving young woman. He allowed her the time to cry and once she managed to pull herself together, he began to question her. He was patient and soft-spoken and it was definitely a side of Mac Callie had never seen before, a side she found very appealing.

"What about men?" Mac now asked. "Do you know if she was seeing anyone?"

"She wasn't seeing anyone at the moment. She was dating Roger Lathrop for a bit, but he got a little too controlling so she broke up with him. It was a pretty bad breakup and since then she's been single," Shelly said tearfully.

"When was the breakup with Roger?" Mac leaned forward in his chair.

"About three weeks ago or so." Her eyes widened. "Do you think he...he killed her?"

"We don't know anything right now. We're just in the beginning stages of the investigation. Do you know anyone Melinda was having a problem with, male or female?" Mac asked.

Shelly shook her head. "No, nobody. Melinda is…was…super easy to get along with. Everybody liked her." Tears filled her eyes once again. "I just can't believe she's gone. I can't believe somebody actually killed her."

"Shelly, we're so sorry about your friend," Callie said. "She was wearing a light blue sweatshirt. Do you know if she changed out of her work T-shirt before she left here yesterday?"

"She always changed into regular street clothes before she left here."

"Did she take her work T-shirt with her?" Callie asked.

Shelly nodded. "She always rolled it up and shoved it into her purse."

"We just want to thank you for speaking to us," Mac said. He stood and pulled a card from his shirt pocket. "If you think of anything that might help us identify the perpetrator, please call me no matter what the time."

Shelly shook her head as tears once again raced down her cheeks. "Is it okay if I go to the restroom?" she asked tearfully.

"I'm sure that would be fine," Callie replied. "Come on, I'll walk with you."

Callie accompanied Shelly to the ladies' room door and then went back to the office, where Mac was once again seated. They spoke to three more waitresses but didn't get any new information to help them fill in the blanks of Melinda's actions throughout the afternoon of her murder.

However, one thing was clear. They needed to interrogate Roger Lathrop and it was something Callie wasn't particularly looking forward to.

"He should be at work now," Mac said once they were back in his car.

Roger had his own insurance business. He worked alone out of an office located a block off Main Street. The tall, blond, attractive man had a reputation as a ladies' man. Callie had never spent any time with him and she doubted he even knew her name. However, she'd definitely heard about his reputation and what she'd heard about him made him unattractive to her.

Besides, her heart was already involved with another man, although that man had no idea how she felt about him. She cast a quick glance at Mac. He looked so handsome even though a frown cut across his forehead and his fingers clenched the steering wheel tightly.

She could only imagine the stress he must be under as the chief lawman for the town with this heinous murder on his hands. He finally pulled up and parked in front of Roger's office. Before he got out of the car, he made several phone calls to check in on the other deputies who were also working on the case.

"Ready to do this?" he asked her once he was off the phone.

"Ready when you are," she replied.

They both exited the car and she grabbed her coat from the back seat and put it on. They were immediately buffeted by the cold wind that had picked up since they'd been in the café. She welcomed the warmth in Roger's office as they stepped inside.

Roger immediately stood from behind a sleek, modern black-and-silver desk. "Sheriff, always a pleasure," he said and walked around the desk to shake Mac's hand.

He then looked at Callie, his blue eyes doing a quick up-and-down even though she was clad in her furry winter coat. "I've seen you around town, but I don't think we've ever officially met." He held out his hand to her.

"Deputy Stevens," she replied and gave his hand a quick shake.

He smiled at her, exposing even white teeth. "Does Deputy Stevens have a first name?"

"Callie," she said reluctantly.

"A pleasure to meet you, Callie. So, what

can I do for you both? Need some kind of insurance?" He looked from Callie to Mac.

"Melinda Tyson was murdered last night," Mac said.

Roger's eyes widened and he took a step backward. "You're kidding me, right? This is some kind of a sick joke, right?" He looked at Callie and then back at Mac. "Please tell me this is a joke."

"No joke," Mac replied tersely. "And we need to ask you some questions starting with where you were last night between the hours of eight and midnight."

Roger walked back to his chair, sank down and then gestured them into the two chairs in front of the desk. "I was home."

"Was anyone with you who can corroborate that?" Mac asked.

"I...no... I was home by myself. I closed up the office at seven, then went home and watched some television and then I went to bed." He shook his head. "I just can't believe this has happened."

"What about between the hours of eleven to one in the afternoon yesterday?"

Roger frowned. "Here. I was here in the office all day, although about one or so I drove through Billy's Burgers to pick up some lunch."

"We understand that recently you had a

pretty volatile breakup with Melinda," Mac continued.

"Volatile…" His eyes widened again. "Wait a minute… Do you think I had something to do with this? You really think I had something to do with her murder?" He released a hoarse bark of laughter. "My God, you've got to be kidding me." He laughed again and shook his head.

"There's nothing funny about this, Roger," Mac said. "Is it true that you were unhappy about Melinda breaking up with you?"

"Well, I wasn't exactly happy about it, but it wasn't like I was madly in love with her. We'd only been dating about a month or so. I certainly wasn't upset enough to feel like murdering her."

Mac continued to ask questions and Callie watched Roger carefully, looking for any tells that might indicate the handsome blond man was lying.

It was hard to tell, especially as he kept casting his gaze to her in what could only be perceived as flirtatiousness. It was not only uncomfortable but it was completely inappropriate and downright sleazy. However, that didn't make him guilty of murder.

Mac finally stood. "You'll be available if

we have any more questions for you at another time?"

"Of course." Roger also got up. "But I can tell you if you think I had anything to do with Melinda's death, then you're barking up the wrong tree." He flashed a smooth smile at Callie. "However, if you want to question me again, please feel free to bring Deputy Callie with you."

Callie expelled a deep breath as they stepped out of the office. "That man is a creep with no boundaries and no social awareness at all," she exclaimed once they were back in the car.

"Yes, but is he a murderer?" Mac started the engine and then turned in his seat to look at her.

"Hard to tell at this point. He looked genuinely shocked when you told him about the murder, but that could be just really good acting."

The conversation was interrupted by Mac's radio going off. "Sheriff, it's Pete. I just thought I'd let you know that last night when Claudia Graham was closing up her shop at around eight, she saw Nathan Brighton doing some work on the store next door. I thought you might want to talk to him in case he saw something important last night."

"Thanks, Pete. You have any idea where Nathan is right now?" Mac asked.

"Sorry, don't have a clue," Pete replied.

"Thanks anyway," Mac said. "We'll hunt him down."

"Surely if Nathan saw the murderer or the body being left last night, he would have called you immediately," Callie said once Mac had hung up.

"You would think so, but knowing he was on the street last night just a couple of hours before Melinda's body was left, means I need to find him and question him," Mac replied. "To be honest, I'm not even sure Nathan has a cell phone. In any case I've never had a number for him. We'll start by going to his house."

"It was awfully cold last night to be working on something so late and outside," she said.

"As far as I know Nathan would take a job in hell if one was offered to him," Mac replied.

Callie laughed. Nathan was the town handyman. He traveled in a rusted old black pickup filled with all kind of tools and equipment for doing almost any odd job anyone would ask of him.

Mac headed back down Main Street. Callie gazed at the clock on the dashboard. It was approaching the time when she'd have to put away her deputy badge and go back on the desk.

"Maybe you need to drop me off at the office," she said. "It's almost time for my shift to begin."

"You aren't going back on the desk," Mac said. "I contacted Dana this morning. She'll be working as a dispatcher through this investigation." He flashed her a quick smile. "As long as you're up for it, you're an unofficial deputy, but you will continue to work only with me."

"Oh Mac, thank you." Happiness filled her. "I swear you won't regret it. I want to learn from you and I'll be the best deputy you could ever ask for."

Maybe…just maybe with enough time he would see her not only as a good deputy but as the loving, caring woman he needed and wanted in his life.

However, first they needed to solve the murder and put a madman away.

Chapter Three

Nathan lived in a very small house on the edge of town. An old barn stood on the property, but it was merely a skeleton of broken boards and a roof that had collapsed in on itself long ago.

The house was definitely not a representation of Nathan's skill as a handyman. The place was badly weathered and begged for fresh paint and the steps leading up to the front door looked positively hazardous.

"It's obvious he isn't here. His truck isn't here," Mac said and drove on by the house. "We'll have to drive around town and see if we can find out where he might be working today."

"I've noticed you haven't mentioned anything about the bird or the hat to anyone we've spoken to. I'm assuming you've told everyone to keep those things under wraps," Callie said.

"Definitely. Aside from the medical examiners, I'm hoping the only people who will know about those things are us and the killer. They will be our secret and if we interview anyone who knows about them, then we'll know we're talking to the murderer."

A chill crawled up her back. "It's hard to believe somebody here in Rock Ridge is capable of that kind of murder...of any kind of murder," she said.

"I guess this is just a reminder that you never know what kind of rage and darkness exists in somebody's mind. Some people only let you see what they want you to see."

"That's frightening to think about, but I know all you have to do is look at the news from bigger cities to know that's true. I just never believed it would be true of somebody here in Rock Ridge."

"There's no way I believe somebody just blew through town last night and randomly killed Melinda," he replied.

"Not with as many stab wounds as she received," Callie agreed. "It would take a lot for me to believe that this was a stranger killer."

"I'm glad we're on the same page," he replied and shot her a quick smile that warmed her more than the heated air flowing out of his car vents.

"When we aren't on the same page, I'll let you know," she replied.

He released a small laugh. "I'm sure you will."

She looked at him curiously. "Surely you wouldn't have it any other way, right? I mean, if I have a different opinion from yours, you should at least hear me out, right?"

"You're right. I wouldn't have it any other way," he replied. "It's important that we all bounce ideas off each other to make sure we remain open to any and all potential perps. Listening to other opinions is how we don't develop tunnel vision."

They fell silent as he drove up and down several streets, looking for Nathan's familiar truck. She drew in the scent in the car, a smell of leather cleaner that mingled with his very attractive cologne.

So far, she'd spent over eight hours with Mac and in those hours, he'd said or done nothing to break the crush…or her insane attraction to him.

She stared at his hand on the steering wheel. He had big hands and for a moment she wondered what it would feel like to have his hands caressing her. She could just imagine those hands doing a slow slide down the length of her naked body. A new warmth swept through her, a warmth that flushed her from head to toe.

"There he is." Mac's voice yanked her from her brief, very hot fantasy.

She looked out the car window and saw Nathan's truck parked against the curb up the street. Mac pulled up behind it and cut the engine. She turned around and grabbed her coat from the back seat.

"Why don't you just wear your coat when you're in the car?" Mac asked as they walked toward the attractive ranch house where apparently Nathan was doing some work.

"I hate wearing a coat in a car. It feels too restrictive and overheats me," she explained as she got into her coat.

"Do I have the heater too warm in the car for you?"

"No, not at all. It's just a little quirk of mine," she replied.

By that time, they had reached the house and Mac knocked on the front door. A man Callie recognized from around town opened the door. "Hey, Simon," Mac said in greeting.

"Mac, come on in out of the cold," he replied and opened the door wider for them to step into a small entryway. Simon smiled and nodded at Callie and then looked back at Mac. "Is something wrong?" His welcoming smile faded and worry shone from his eyes.

"No, not at all," Mac replied. "We just need to speak to Nathan and we saw his truck outside."

Simon pointed down the hallway. "He's painting our spare bedroom. It's the second door on the right."

Callie followed behind Mac and when they reached the correct door, he gave a quick knock and then opened the door. The room was empty of furniture and two windows were open to vent the odor of fresh paint.

Nathan looked at them in surprise. "Sheriff, what are you doing here?" Nathan was a medium-sized man, more wiry than bulky. He had a round face and wide brown eyes that exuded an innocence of spirit.

"Hi, Nathan. We have a few questions for you about what you were doing on Main Street last night," Mac said.

Nathan placed his paint roller back into the tray and then looked at Mac again. "I was replacing some rotted wood on the bottom of the door to Trisha's Trinkets. Why? Did I do something wrong?" He eyed Mac worriedly.

"No, but I was just wondering why you

were working that late in the evening," Mac replied.

"Trisha wanted it fixed after-hours, so I did it as soon as she shut down her shop for the night."

"And what time was that?" Mac asked.

Nathan frowned. "Around seven o'clock or so."

"And how long did it take you to complete your work?"

"Oh, about a half an hour. Why?" He glanced from Mac to Callie and then back again.

"So, did you immediately leave the area once you were finished with your work?" Mac asked.

"It was too cold and nobody was around to hang out with me, so I went right home," Nathan replied.

"Then you didn't see anyone out and about?"

As she had with Roger, Callie tried to see if she saw any signs of lying emanating from Nathan, but he was difficult to read with his innocent eyes and slightly slack features.

"Do you have a cell phone, Nathan? I thought maybe you could give me your number," Mac said.

"Oh, I don't have one of those cell phones. They seem way too complicated to me. But

I do have a home phone. It's got an answering machine and everything." Nathan smiled broadly. "I can give you that number."

It took only a few more questions for them to figure out that either Nathan had seen nothing suspicious the night before or he knew more than he was telling and was responsible for Melinda's murder.

"What do you think?" she asked once they were in the car again.

"Hard to tell," Mac replied.

"No offense, but is Nathan bright enough to pull something like this off? I mean, our killer managed somehow to take Melinda off the streets, go to a place where he killed her and then pose her on Main Street and he got away without anyone seeing him. Nathan seems to be just a little slow. He thinks cell phones are too hard."

"Yeah, Nathan wouldn't be on the top of my list of suspects. Whoever killed Melinda was smart. It took a lot of planning and calculation to pull this off." Mac released a deep sigh.

"So, what's next?"

"We need to start pounding the sidewalks and talking to people. We need to find out if anyone saw Melinda after her shift ended yesterday or if anyone saw a vehicle or a person in or around the post office between nine and midnight last night." He cast her a quick glance. "You know there's nothing glamorous about a murder investigation."

She looked at him in surprise and then laughed. "What makes you think I'm looking for anything glamorous?"

"Sometimes people watch the shows on television about investigating a murder and they don't realize it's a lot of hard work. It's long hours and walking the streets and talking to people."

"Mac, I want to put in that work. My only goal is to do whatever it takes to put this murderer away," she replied. "Besides, you didn't answer my question. What would make you think I'm looking for glamour?"

"I don't know—you always dress really nice and look a little bit glamorous when you come in to work the desk," he said after a long hesitation.

She stared at his profile as a warm flutter raced through her chest. So he *had* noticed her... He'd really noticed her.

"Thank you for the compliment, but honestly, Mac, if I was looking for glamour, I would have stayed in Kansas City, which has far more opportunities for glamour than Rock Ridge. Trust me, I'm right where I want to be and working with you is exactly what I've wanted to do."

He pulled into a parking space on one end of Main Street and turned off the car. "We'll start here. We need to speak to all the people in the stores and on the street. I want to know if anyone saw Melinda yesterday after her shift or if anyone saw a person or a vehicle lingering around the bench around the time Melinda's body was left there."

As they got out of the car, Callie was still processing the fact that Mac had noticed how she dressed, how she looked when she came into work. The other dispatchers usually wore sweats and sweatshirts, but that just wasn't Callie's style. She always dressed up a bit for work, and she was thrilled that her boss...the man she had a major crush on... hadn't been oblivious of the fact.

For the next three hours they went in and out of the stores, asking questions of anyone they came across. Callie was surprised by how Mac seemed to know everyone. He asked about kids by name and had the ability to put everyone at ease as he spoke to them.

Still, even with his personable approach they came up empty-handed. Nobody had seen Melinda during the afternoon the day before and nobody they spoke to had seen anything around the time that Melinda's body had been found.

It was six thirty when he drove through a hamburger place and they each ordered dinner. Callie was starving, having only had a bagel and coffee that morning and no lunch.

They took their burgers back to the office, where Mac had called a meeting of all his deputies. There were fourteen men who made up the sum of the Rock Ridge law enforcement team.

There were still a few missing from the round tables in the break room. Callie and Mac began to eat their cheeseburgers and fries as they waited for the remaining deputies to show up.

The men were unusually subdued. Mac ate quickly and when all the men were there, he began to speak to them about the murder and what little information they had gleaned that day.

Unfortunately, most of the deputies who had been working that day hadn't come up with any information that would move the investigation forward, either.

It was Deputy Dwight Mayfield who had a new name. "I heard from Derek Bowman that he was making a run to the grocery store last night around eight and saw Ben Kincaid on the sidewalk near the post office."

"Did he say what Ben was doing?" Mac asked.

"Knowing Ben, he was probably talking to the spirits or chanting to the gods of the wind," Johnny said wryly.

Ben Kincaid was definitely the town's eccentric. He not only believed in ghosts, but he also believed that people from another planet walked among them and that there were good spirits and bad ones. Had he believed that Melinda was one of the bad spirits who needed to be killed?

"As you can see, Callie has joined our team," Mac said after a few more questions and discussion among everyone.

The razzing began immediately as they all teased her. But the teasing was cut short as Mac then continued. "You all know what I need from you, and remember that we're keeping the bird and the hat information away from the public," Mac said as he finished up the meeting.

"If that information leaks out, trust me I won't rest until I know who leaked it and that person will be immediately fired. Now, get back on the streets if you're on duty and if you aren't on duty then I recommend you go home and get as much rest as you can. This investigation will require that you're all on the top of your game and since we're such a small force, I may need you all working overtime," Mac finished.

"So, are we on our way to talk to Ben," Callie asked once the men were all gone.

Mac looked at her in surprise. "I just assumed you'd be ready to call it a day. You've been going pretty hard at it since early this morning."

"There's still a potential suspect to interrogate. I'll be through for the day when you are." She got up from the table, threw her fast-food trash away and then grabbed her coat. "Shall we?"

Minutes later they were back in his car and headed to wherever Ben lived. "I've seen Ben before out and around on the streets. Has he always been…uh…strange?" Callie asked.

Mac laughed, the low, deep rumble setting off another wave of pleasant heat through her. "I went to grade school and high school with Ben, and for as long as I've known him, he's been pretty odd."

When Mac got to the end of the main drag, he turned left and then turned left again, taking them out to the very edge of town. He then made a right turn on a gravel road and after ten minutes or so he pulled into the driveway of Ben's house.

"Interesting," Callie said as she looked at Ben's home. There were about a dozen yard lights illuminating not only the small ranch house, but also the entire yard, which appeared to be surrounded by woods.

There were half a dozen trees on the property and not only did dozens of wind chimes hang from the branches, but there were also strange little stuffed figures and other odd items.

When they got out of the car the discordant sound of all the chimes clanging together filled the air. Several lights shone from the inside and an old maroon Buick she assumed to be Ben's car was in the driveway.

Mac knocked on the front door and Ben answered. He was a short man with shaggy black hair and intense green eyes. "Sheriff, don't tell me you got another complaint about the things I have in my yard."

"No, nothing like that," Mac replied. "Can we come in? It's rather hard to hear out here."

Ben hesitated a moment and then opened the door wider to allow them to enter. Inside, things were as strange as they were outside.

There was a futon shoved against one wall and a television was mounted on the opposite wall. That's where all normalcy stopped. The walls were covered with pictures of big-eyed aliens and angry demons. There were statues of angels and strange creatures on the coffee and end tables.

He gestured them to the futon, but Mac remained standing and Callie stayed at Mac's side. "Ben, we won't be here long. I just have a few questions for you."

Ben's eyes were scary intense as he stared unblinkingly at Mac. "Questions about what?"

"I understand you were out and about on Main Street last night," Mac said.

Ben's gaze shot to Callie and then back at Mac. "Is that a crime?"

"Of course not," Mac replied. "We had a body of a murder victim show up on the bench in front of the post office. Since you were in the general area not long before that happened, we were just wondering what you were doing there."

"Ah, that explains it," Ben said with a knowing shake of his head.

"Explains what?"

"I picked up a couple things at the grocery store and had a sudden feeling that something evil was coming to Main Street. I walked up and down the center of the sidewalks and stopped occasionally to say a prayer in an attempt to keep the evil away. Unfortunately, from what you just told me my prayers were too late."

"Did you see anything unusual while you were out there?" Mac asked. Callie wondered if Ben would even recognize anything considered unusual.

The man had a restless energy about him. His fingers moved against each other constantly and a tic appeared at the outward corner of his right eye. Were these things normal or were they an unconscious signal of guilt?

Mac asked him several more questions, but Ben had little to add. According to him he'd been in his home all day the day before until he'd left in the evening to go to the grocery store. He professed not only to not seeing Melinda. He said he didn't even know for sure who she was.

"He is definitely one strange man," Callie said once they were back in the car and headed back to town.

"Yeah, but is he our man?"

Callie heard the weariness and frustration in Mac's voice. She felt some of that herself. After the first day of the investigation, they had nothing to go on. They had some ifs and maybes but nothing concrete to follow up on to find Melinda's murderer.

He remained silent on the drive to her house. She sensed it was the heavy silence of mental weariness. "I'll see you tomorrow," he said once he was parked at her curb.

Without any thought, she reached out and covered one of his hands with hers. "We'll get him, Mac. We're going to get this guy and make sure he goes to jail."

He was quiet for a long moment and then pulled his hand from beneath hers. "That's the goal," he replied.

There was an awkward pause between them and then with a murmured goodbye, Callie got out, grabbed her coat from the back seat and then headed up her sidewalk.

She unlocked her front door and then turned to wave at Mac, who slowly pulled away from the curb. She went inside and tossed her coat across the top of the sofa.

It was stupid to be disappointed that they hadn't solved the murder in a single day. This was going to probably be a marathon rather than a sprint.

Still, she couldn't help but feel a little depressed by the utter lack of any real leads. Even though it had been a long day, she wasn't quite ready to go to bed. She needed to relax and unwind a bit before heading to sleep.

She stared at the Christmas tree she'd put up

a couple of nights before. All the trimmings were in boxes on the floor next to the bare tree. Maybe now was a good time to do a little work to turn it into a real, decorated piece of work.

As she began to string the lights, thoughts of the family she'd lost filled her head. A little over two years ago her father and mother and younger sister had all perished when their car had been struck by a drunk driver.

It was a tragedy that still haunted her and it was what had brought her back to her family home in Rock Ridge. She could have sold the house and moved back to Kansas City, but in the end, she couldn't do it.

Memories of laughter and joyous moments filled this house. It was warm and inviting and Callie could easily envision raising her children here. All she needed was that special man. She'd thought she'd found him in Mac.

However, before she could tell or show him how she felt about him she had to be the best deputy he'd ever had.

Chapter Four

Mac woke at a little after five after suffering sleep filled with nightmares. He'd dreamed of giant bobtail quail chasing Callie down a darkened street. It sounded ridiculous, but it had been terrifying. The quail had angry eyes and sharp beaks and he'd known their intent was to lodge in her mouth to strangle her to death.

He'd chased after Callie, yelling for her not to scream, not to even open her mouth at all. He'd pulled his gun to shoot the murderous birds, but when he shot, he realized his gun was filled with blanks.

He now sat at his kitchen table with a cup of coffee and all his notes from the day before in front of him. He needed to concentrate on the paperwork rather than the dream and the woman at the center of it.

Still, it was thoughts of Callie that intruded in his mind. She'd surprised him with her intelligence and her work ethic…at least on her first day. It was possible she'd pushed herself yesterday in an effort to make a good impression on him and that work ethic would change as the days went on.

It wasn't how hard she worked that worried him as much as it was the evocative scent of her perfume, her ready, beautiful smile and positive attitude. Even now with a new day dawning his hand still seemed to hold the imprint of her small, warm hand on top of his.

He was definitely drawn to her, but it wouldn't be fair to her for him to act on it, as he knew there was no future for her with him. He was confident that as they worked together, he could keep things completely professional with her.

What he really needed at the moment was something…anything…that would help him solve the case. He finally got up from the table and headed into his bathroom to take a shower.

He'd moved into this small apartment three years before, when his world had exploded and he'd needed to escape the house that held far too many memories, memories both good and bad.

He was comfortable in the small one-bedroom space that was furnished minimally. Besides, he really only showered and slept here. He spent most of his time at the sheriff's office.

A half an hour later he was on his way to work, his mind whirling with suppositions and theories. Why would somebody shove a dead bird into Melinda's mouth? The bird had to be important in the psyche of the killer. But why? He felt like if they could solve that, then they'd know who the murderer was. But how did you solve crazy?

When he'd seen the weather report that morning, he'd learned this unusual cold had settled in for good through the holidays and there were several chances for snow in the coming days. He already longed for the spring.

He entered the back door and stopped in the break room. Callie sat at one of the tables, a cup of coffee before her and reading something on her cell phone. There were little gaily decorated plastic Christmas trees in the center of each round table.

"Good morning, Callie."

She jumped at the sound of his voice. She shot a quick glance at the Christmas tree on her table and then looked up at him. "Good morning, Mac."

He looked at all the trees and then looked back at her. "What are you, the Christmas elf?"

She released what sounded like a nervous laugh. "I'm just trying to counteract your grinchlike nature."

There was no way he intended to share with her that anything Christmas related brought back bad memories of loss and anger and pain and betrayal.

However, he had noticed over the past year that some of those negative memories had begun to dull and no longer hurt as badly as they once had.

"Are you going to make me pack up all these happy little trees? Are you going to take away my joy, everyone else's joy of Christmas?" she asked. She raised her chin and held his gaze intently.

He had to give it to her; she had more guts than the men who worked for him, he thought. In the past three years nobody had challenged him about his no-Christmas policy.

"No, I'm not," he replied. "Now, I'll be in my office for the next half an hour or so and then we're going to hit the streets once again."

Minutes later he was seated at his desk. There would be few people out and about in town at this time of the morning and in any case, he already had four deputies actively working the streets. But he knew they'd probably have little to report after another cold December night.

So far, the evidence they had gathered around the bench had yielded no clues. He hadn't really expected it to. Right now, Roger Lathrop was at the top of his suspect list. The smooth insurance salesman had a volatile history with the victim in the recent past and that made him a definite person of interest.

Ben Kincaid was a close second, only in that the man had so many strange ideas and the fact that he'd been out on Main Street around the time that Melinda's body had been found.

And there was still a question as to where Melinda had been killed. According to the autopsy report she'd lost a lot of blood. So, where was that blood? It hadn't been around the bench. Was it in somebody's spare room or had it been washed down a bathtub drain? Unfortunately, he didn't have any evidence to take to a judge to get a search warrant for anywhere.

He glanced at the clock on the wall. Seven thirty on the second day of a murder investigation and already he felt discouraged.

He would be the first person to say he'd had an easy run since becoming sheriff seven years before. He'd been twenty-six years old when he'd become the head lawman in the small town.

In the past seven years there had been bar fights and petty thefts, neighborly disputes and speeders. He'd had one domestic dispute that had tragically ended in a murder, but other than that he'd never been tested in the way he knew this murder would test him.

And so far, he felt like he was failing.

At eight o'clock he rose and grabbed his coat for another day of walking the streets and talking to the people of his town. When he went back into the break room several of the deputies who had come off duty were there along with Callie.

They were all involved in a lively discussion about various serial killers of the past. He stood in the doorway and listened to them for several minutes. He was lucky his team was built with strong, intelligent people who all worked together for the same common goal…to live in a town where law and order ruled the day.

"All right, people. Thankfully we aren't chasing a serial killer right now. You men who just got off work need to go home and get some sleep, and Callie, it's time to hit the streets again," he said.

Callie immediately got to her feet and went to the rack to grab her coat. The other men got up more slowly, wearing their weariness after their shifts visibly in their slowness of movements.

"I did some more research last night," Callie said once they were in the patrol car.

"Was that before or after you packed up all those little Christmas trees to bring to work?" he asked with a sideways glance at her.

"It was after. Do you intend to subtly punish me all day for those trees?" she asked.

He released a short laugh. "No, I have far more important things on my mind." In fact, he'd realized the decorations in the office didn't bother him too much. At least when he got home at night there were no items of the approaching holiday there to distract him.

"Why do you hate Christmas so much?"

Her question took him by surprise, but there was no way he intended to answer it. At heart Mac was a very private person. He didn't share personal things about his life with anyone. Besides, Callie was really a stranger to him.

"It's a long story and we don't have time to talk about Christmas or my personal feelings about it right now. I'm far more interested in what you researched last night."

"I did a search for the phrase 'bird in the mouth.'"

"Ha, I doubt that yielded anything," he replied.

"Actually, to my utter surprise I got two hits. The first one was a poem that I didn't really understand and the second one was a short story that was a bit bizarre. I read them both very carefully, but I don't think they have anything to do with our murderer."

"Can you write down the references and give them to me?"

"Absolutely." She pulled a small notebook and pen from her purse and wrote for a minute, ripped off the page and then set it on the console between them. "Maybe you can get something out of them that I missed. I'm just not the literary type. I'm a simple girl who likes my poem to rhyme."

He smiled wryly. "If you couldn't make sense of the references then I doubt I'll have any better luck. I'm just a small-town sheriff and I like my poetry to rhyme, too."

He felt the warmth of her gaze on him. "So, what's on our agenda for today?" she asked.

He released a deep sigh. "Same as yesterday. We talk to people we haven't talked to yet to see if anyone saw anything on the night Melinda's body was left on the bench. I can't help but think there has to be somebody who might have seen a vehicle parked there around that time. We also need to try to find anyone who saw Melinda at any point after she got off work."

"At least it isn't quite as blustery today as it was yesterday," she said. "The more people we speak to, the better our odds that we'll find somebody who saw something."

There was such an optimism in her voice and he found that optimism appealing. He was finding a lot of things about Callie Stevens appealing. He tightened his hands on his steering wheel, as if it might protect him from his own growing lust where she was concerned.

And he definitely had a growing case of lust that was building with every minute he spent with her. Each time he smelled her scent, or listened to the low, sexy sound of her voice, his desire for her grew.

Maybe he should have kept her on the desk. At least that way he'd only see her briefly a couple times a day. But what kind of a man would he be to stop her ambition just because she made him uncomfortable? She deserved to be in the seat next to him.

She was intelligent and sharp and had already proved to him that she belonged playing an active role in the investigation.

He was just going to have to get over his attraction to her. However, right now that seemed as difficult as catching a killer.

IT HAD BEEN another long day of pounding the pavement and talking to people. Finally, at seven o'clock they knocked off to have dinner at the café.

"Well, today was a waste of time," Mac said as they sat in a booth toward the back of the café. His eyes were the color of turbulent storm clouds.

"It might feel that way right now, but at least we know now who didn't see anything the night of Melinda's murder," Callie replied. "In the process of elimination, we're making progress."

"Do you always see the bright side of things?" One of his dark brows rose up quizzically.

"It's a flaw of mine," she replied with a half smile. "My mother used to say I could find something positive at a funeral."

To her sudden surprise, a burst of emotion rose up inside her at thoughts of her family. Tears misted her eyes and she quickly stared down at the wooden tabletop.

"Callie, I've never told you how very sorry I am about you losing your family, especially to a drunk driver." He reached out and covered one of her hands with his. "It wasn't fair and it wasn't right and I'm really sorry about your loss." He pulled his hand away but not before she gained strength from the comforting warmth of his touch.

She drew in a deep breath to tamp down the unexpected emotions and then looked up at him. "Thanks, Mac. I won't lie—it was the absolute worst time in my life. But after I got through the initial shock and grief, I realized it was important that I celebrate them instead of mourn them."

The conversation halted as a waitress came to their table to take their order. Mac ordered the meatloaf platter and Callie a bacon cheeseburger and fries. They both opted for sodas.

"That's why Christmas is so important to me," Callie continued once the waitress left the table. "My mother loved the holiday. All my memories of Christmas are of warmth and happiness and love, and that's what I intend to have in my home this year."

"Then I hope that's what you have," he replied. "I'm wondering if we need to reinterview Roger at his home and see if he tells us the same story about his relationship with Melinda as he did before. Some of her friends that we've spoken to have indicated the relationship was more volatile than Roger let on."

She wasn't lost to the fact that he'd intentionally changed the subject. But they were in the middle of a murder investigation and she understood he probably wasn't really interested in her personal life.

"I don't even know where Roger lives," she replied.

"He owns a house right here on Main Street. It's a nice two-story like your place."

"Too bad we can't get a warrant to search it from top to bottom. So far he's the best suspect we have."

"I agree, but I can't go to a judge and tell him we think he might be guilty because almost a month before, he dated the victim. We need something more concrete than that for a search warrant to be granted." His frown returned to etch lines across his forehead, lines that did nothing to detract from his attractiveness.

At that moment the waitress returned with their meals and drinks. "Anything else I can do for you?" she asked.

"No, I think we're good," Mac said. The waitress left to attend to other diners.

"It's obvious from all our questioning of people that nobody saw Melinda after she stopped working. All I can think of is when her shift ended and she walked outside, there must have been somebody in a car, somebody she would trust to get into their car," she said.

"And the logical person would be Roger," Mac said.

Callie shrugged and then grabbed a fry and dragged it through a pool of ketchup. "Maybe he pulled up and told her they needed to talk…that he was still interested in her and wanted a reconciliation."

"Maybe," Mac agreed. "But we're a small town. There might be somebody else who she'd trust to get into their car. Hell, we don't even know for sure that the killer is a male."

"I just assumed it was a male by the strength shown in the stab wounds," she replied.

"An enraged woman could have made those wounds," Mac said. "We have to keep an open mind with this case."

"But Shelly told us she didn't have any problems with anyone…that she was well-liked among all the women who work here. If I was having an issue with somebody, my best friend would know about it and I believe that would be the case between Shelly and Melinda."

"So, that brings us back to square one. However, I do believe Melinda got into somebody's car outside here and that somebody took her to a place, held her for hours and then killed her."

For the next few minutes, they ate in silence. Unanswered questions whirled around in Callie's head. Who had picked up Melinda after she'd finished her shift here? Was Mac ever going to notice her as a woman? Where had Melinda been murdered? Was she being stupid to believe that Mac could ever fall in love with her?

They were halfway through their meal when Mac began talking again. "I keep trying to figure out how the killer managed to get hold of a bobtail quail. Birds aren't exactly the easiest creatures to catch and those birds in particular have good camouflage."

"Is there anyone in town who raises birds?" she asked.

Mac shook his head. "Not that I've ever heard about."

"Maybe we should speak to Craig Olson at the pet store," she suggested. "He might know any breeders in the area."

"Dammit." Mac slammed his hand down on the table.

His outburst caused her to jump in surprise. "What?"

He must have realized he'd startled her. He offered her a slightly sheepish smile. "I'm just mad because I didn't think about talking to Craig until you just now brought it up."

"Mac, give yourself a break. It isn't like you've been in your office lounging around and playing video games since the murder occurred. You've been working your butt off." And a fine butt it was, she mentally added.

"I have to say I've been surprised and impressed that you're putting in the hours with me."

"The minute I saw Melinda, I knew I'd work as long and as hard as I could to put away her killer. I hope you'll consider me your right-hand man, or in this case, your right-hand woman."

This time he offered her a real warm smile. "Thank you, Callie. I appreciate it. I appreciate your thoughts and opinions as this case continues."

She nodded and began to eat once again. Oh, when he smiled at her like that, with his eyes a warm smoky gray and his features all relaxed, she wanted to jump into his arms and feel his closeness.

She wanted to see his sexy, smoky eyes light up with desire for her. She wanted to feel his big strong arms around her. More than anything she wanted him to love her.

Maybe this case and spending so much time with Mac was making her a little bit crazy. She definitely had a crush on him, but a crush was a long way from real true love.

Her thoughts about Mac might be getting away from her because, despite what she had told him about the joys of Christmas, this year she felt a loneliness she hadn't really experienced before.

One day at a time, she reminded herself. One way or another her feelings toward Mac would work themselves out and one way or another she was determined to have a wonderful Christmas even if she was all alone again.

They had just finished eating and were in the process of leaving the café when Allen Wilson bumped into them as they stepped out the door.

"Sheriff…just the person I need to see." Allen grabbed hold of Mac's forearm. Allen's eyes were wide and he was half-breathless. "I… I knew a parking spot would be hard to find in front of the café so I… I parked on th-the other side of the center park and w-walked over. But…there's a dead body in the park."

Chapter Five

Mac's heart crashed to the ground at Allen's words. What the hell? A body in the park? He pulled the man completely outside of the café. "Could you tell who it is?"

"I think it's Candy Waltrip, but I'm not positive," Allen replied, his eyes still big with obvious shock.

"Where exactly in the park is she?" Mac's head reeled with dread.

"You know the bench next to that big oak tree? She's there," Allen said. "I've… I've never seen somebody dead like that before. At first, I thought she was just sitting there, but I got a little closer and her eyes were wide open…just staring and I realized she was… she was dead." He released a deep gasp. "It's bad, Sheriff… It's really bad."

"Allen…" Mac pulled him away from the café front door. "I'm going to ask you a big favor," he said. "If you still intend to go inside and have dinner, could you not tell anyone about this? The last thing I need right now is a crowd to gather around the scene."

"To be honest, I don't feel much like eating right now. I think I'll just head back home," Allen replied.

"You'll be at home if I need to talk to you later?" Mac asked.

"I'll be there."

"Thanks, Allen, and I'm sorry you had to be a part of this." Mac clapped the man on the back. "And I appreciate you keeping this quiet for now."

Minutes later Allen had left and, after grabbing high-power flashlights and protective gear from Mac's trunk, he and Callie began to walk from the café to the park bench Allen had indicated.

"I can't believe this is happening," he said tersely.

"Surely it's not the same," Callie replied. "Hopefully this is the result of some sort of accident or a medical emergency of some kind."

It wasn't the result of any accident or a medical emergency. Mac gazed toward the body in the distance and the first thing he saw was a small Santa hat on Candy's blond hair. He couldn't stop the groan that rose up from the very depths of him.

Before getting any closer, he and Callie stopped to put on booties and gloves and then they approached the body. It wasn't quite the same. Instead of a dead bird in her mouth, Candy held a dead bird in each hand. And yet it was the same.

She wore the light blue T-shirt with the café logo on the front. It was what all the waitresses wore when working there. It was obvious she had been stabbed numerous times and was beyond any medical help.

Mac called all his deputies in. Bright lights were set up and the coroner was contacted. Onlookers began to gather and some of the deputies kept them away while others worked to process the scene. Mac conducted the action, ever aware of Callie at his side.

There was an odd sense of comfort in knowing she was just as shocked, just as appalled as he was and in the fact that he knew she and the rest of his team would do anything possible to help him solve these crimes.

He was aware of Callie watching everything. She directed questions to the deputies and the coroner and took copious notes that he knew she'd share with him later. She showed no weariness; rather her high energy was contagious. She was quickly proving herself to be a ride-or-die kind of partner.

When Candy's body was finally taken away, and the birds had been tagged and bagged, Mac and Callie went over the bench with a fine-tooth comb, hoping to find something, anything, that might point to the killer.

Fortunately, his team had done a good job and there was nothing left to collect. Once again there was also no blood, indicating she'd been killed elsewhere. While his deputies continued to process the scene, Mac and Callie headed back to the café.

Once more, he found himself facing Jimmy in his small office. "I heard that somebody is dead in the park," Jimmy said, his broad features radiating concern.

"That somebody is Candy Waltrip," Mac replied.

"My God, what in the hell is going on?" Jimmy asked and shook his head. "Who in the hell is killing off my waitresses?"

The question caught Mac by surprise. He'd been so deep in his own head about the fact that there had been another murder with the victim having birds at the scene that he hadn't had time to look at the bigger picture that had potentially emerged with this newest murder.

Two dead waitresses. Was it possible the answer to the murders rested here in the café?

"So, who have you ticked off lately, Jimmy?" Mac asked. He knew the owner of the café had a reputation for having a pretty bad temper.

Jimmy leaned back in his chair, wiped a hand across his bald pate and frowned. "I had to fire that no-count Ralph Marsten, but that was about three weeks ago. I doubt he could pull together a murder scheme any more than he could figure out how to efficiently work a mop."

"How did he take the news that he was fired?"

"Well, he wasn't happy about it, but he was fond of all the waitresses and I can't imagine him getting some kind of sick revenge on me by killing any of them. He and his wife have been in a couple of times to eat since I fired him and he doesn't seem to be holding a grudge."

"Is there any diner you can think of who might have had an issue with both of the women?" Mac asked.

"None, both of them were well-liked by everyone they waited on. They were friendly, hardworking young women." Jimmy released a deep sigh. "I just can't believe this. I do know this…both of them at one time or another dated that snake oil salesman, Roger Lathrop. Maybe you should talk to that slick creep."

"Oh, trust me, we will," Cassie spoke up for the first time. "Do you know when Roger dated Candy?"

"I think it was right before he dated Melinda. The two used to joke together and say they were members of the Roger the Creep Club."

"What shift did Candy work today?" Mac asked.

"She worked a midshift from ten to two." Jimmy frowned once again. "If either of these women were murdered because of something I said or did, I'll never be able to forgive myself."

"Don't start beating yourself up right now," Mac replied. "We need to solve these murders and figure out what the motive really is." Mac got up with a sense of urgency. "We'll be in and out of here over the next several days interviewing all of your employees. If you think of anything else, Jimmy, please give me a call."

"You know I will," Jimmy replied. He rose from his chair and walked Cassie and Mac out the café's front door.

They immediately headed to the Waltrips' home, where they delivered the news that destroyed another family. Callie was quiet when they returned to the car. He figured she was feeling as bad as he was about the notification they'd just made.

"Where are we going?" She finally broke the silence between them as he headed to the outskirts of town.

"Although my gut instinct tells me Ralph Marsten has nothing to do with any of this, we need to question him so I'm headed to his place now."

"At least we have a bit of direction right now. I can't believe it's just a coincidence that two women who work at the café have been murdered. Somebody has to have some sort of grudge against Jimmy," she said.

"Yeah, tomorrow I intend to push Jimmy harder to think of somebody he's had trouble with," Mac replied. "Jimmy sometimes pops off to someone in a fit of anger and it's possible he popped off to the wrong person."

"I've been in the café when he's hollered at somebody for complaining about his cooking. However, I kind of just assumed everyone took Jimmy with a grain of salt."

Mac tightened his hands on the steering wheel. "But it's possible somebody didn't." He racked his brain to think of somebody, anybody who would harbor such hatred toward the owner of the café.

Had Jimmy somehow stiffed somebody financially? Maybe a supplier or somebody else he did business with? Mac made a mental note to get a list from Jimmy of everyone who he dealt with on that end of the café.

"I still don't know what to make of the birds," Callie said. "The ones Candy was holding in her hands looked like ordinary pigeons."

"That reminds me tomorrow we need to talk to Craig Olson down at the pet shop to see if he knows anyone in the area who raises domestic birds," he said. "We also need to question again all the staff at the café."

"I can't believe we have a second one so quickly after the first," Callie said softly.

He shot her a quick glance. "I can't believe it, either, but here we are."

He turned down a long drive that led to the Marsten home. Ralph and his wife, Rebecca, had lived in the small ranch house for as long as Mac could remember. They had raised their two boys here. Both now lived outside of town, but visited often.

For years Ralph had worked as a janitor at the grade school. He'd retired from that a year ago and since then had been working part-time at the café.

Lights from inside the house shone out into the night and Ralph's car was parked in front. Mac and Callie got out and headed for the front door.

Rebecca answered Mac's knock. She was a diminutive woman with long gray hair she wore in a thick braid down her back. Her blue eyes widened at the sight of Mac. "Sheriff," she greeted him and opened her door wider to allow him and Callie inside.

They entered into the living room, where Ralph sat on the sofa. He was clad in a royal blue robe and stood to greet Mac with a handshake. He nodded to Callie and then gestured for them to have a seat.

"What's going on?" Ralph asked once they were all settled on the sofa and in chairs.

"Where were you about two hours ago?" Mac asked.

Ralph frowned. "I was right here. I've been home all day... Why?" He looked from Mac to Callie and then back to Mac.

"Rebecca, you can confirm that he's been home all day?" Mac asked.

"I can. In fact, he's been underfoot for the last couple of days," she replied. "Please, Sheriff, tell us what's going on?"

"We heard Jimmy fired you, Ralph," Mac said.

Ralph laughed. "He fired me right after I told him I quit. That man doesn't know how to talk to people. I got tired of him yelling at me that I was slow and stupid. I took it and took it and I finally had enough. Since then, I've just been hanging around home and driving my wife crazy." He cast a fond smile to Rebecca.

"Now, would you please tell us why you're here and asking all these questions?" Rebecca asked.

"Candy Waltrip was murdered tonight," Mac replied.

Both Ralph and Rebecca gasped in obvious surprise. "Oh, that poor girl," Rebecca said. "But why are you talking to us about it?"

"Candy makes the second waitress from the café that has been murdered, so we're questioning anyone who might hold a grudge against Jimmy," Mac explained.

"And you thought I…" Ralph's voice trailed off as he stared at Mac. He then shook his head. "Mac, my life is too damned short to hold any kind of a grudge with anyone."

"That's kind of what I figured, Ralph. But I had to do my due diligence in talking to you." Mac stood.

He'd been doubtful all along that Ralph was capable of committing most any crime. Rebecca wasn't the kind of woman who would lie even for her husband. If she said

Ralph had been home the last couple of days, he believed her.

Within minutes he and Callie were back in the car. "I knew that would be a bust," he said as they headed back into town.

"But you still needed to check it out," she replied. "And now we're headed where?"

"Lathrop's place. Even though it's getting late I think it's a perfect time to pop in on him." He cast her a quick glance. As always, he couldn't help but notice how pretty she looked in the illumination from the dashboard. "I'm sure no matter what the time he'll be happy to see Deputy Callie."

"Ugh, don't remind me," she replied.

Mac had to confess, Roger flirting with Callie the last time they'd all spoken hadn't sat well with him. And he consciously didn't want to examine why.

Instead, he thought about the two murdered women…women who were crying out for justice and right now he had no idea how to find it for them.

And with each day that passed, he knew their cries would only get louder in his head.

WHEN MAC PULLED into the driveway of Roger's house, Callie steeled herself for seeing the smooth-talking creep again. Even though she wasn't impressed with Roger Lathrop, she had to admit that his two-story house was quite attractive.

Painted a light gray with darker gray trim, the house also sported two red flowered lounge chairs on the porch that looked welcoming. The place showed way more class than Roger did.

Together she and Mac got out of the car and approached the front door. Despite it being almost midnight, a light shone from the front window.

Roger answered Mac's second knock. "Sheriff, what are you doing here?"

"We need to ask you a few more questions. Can we come in?" Mac asked.

Roger hesitated a moment. "It's awfully late. I was just about to go to bed."

"We were driving by and saw your lights on," Mac replied. "We won't keep you for long." Still Roger hesitated. "Are you going to invite us in or do we have to conduct our interview out here in the cold? Or maybe you'd prefer to come down to the office and answer questions there?"

Roger opened his door to allow them entry. He was clad in a white T-shirt and a pair of navy flannel sleep pants. The living room held a black sofa and love seat and sleek metal-and-glass coffee table and end tables.

An undecorated Christmas tree stood in one corner. On the hardwood floor in front of it several boxes spilled tinsel and a tangle of lights. However, what Callie noticed instantly was a faint smell of bleach in the air.

"Have you been cleaning something?" Mac asked, apparently noticing the same smell.

"Uh, not really. I washed a load of whites a little while ago," Roger replied.

"Your home is very nice," Callie said. "I've always wondered about these grand two-story homes here on Main Street. Would you mind giving me a tour?" She forced a friendly smile to her lips.

"Yeah, I guess I can do that as long as you keep smiling at me like that," he replied and then winked at her.

Callie wanted to throw up, but she kept the smile on her face as he walked them through the front room and into a large, airy kitchen and dining room. The laundry room was right off the kitchen and the smell of bleach seemed to waft in the air from there.

He then took them upstairs to see the three bedrooms and bath. "Thank you for the tour, Roger," she said as they returned to the living room.

"If you're looking for a murder scene here, you're looking in the wrong place," Roger said jokingly.

"What makes you think we'd be looking for a crime scene here?" Mac asked.

"Because last time I met Deputy Callie, I made it my business to find out where she lives. I just happen to know she lives in a two-story house pretty much like this one." He grinned at Callie. "Don't worry, I would never hold the little white lie that you always wondered what a house like this looked like on the inside against a pretty little lady like you."

Despite her irritation with him, she couldn't help the guilty warmth that swept into her cheeks at being called out. It was true that her family home had the same floor plan as Roger's place. It was also creepy that he'd gone to the trouble to find out where she lived.

Roger gestured for them to have a seat on the black sofa and then he sat in a chair facing them. "So, what's going on? Why are you here?" he asked. "More questions about me and Melinda?"

"Actually, we're here to ask you about your relationship with Candy Waltrip," Mac said.

Roger's eyebrows shot up in surprise.

"Candy? I don't have any kind of a relationship with her."

"But you had one in the past," Mac said.

"Months ago… Why? Has something happened to her?"

"Who broke up with who when you and Candy stopped seeing each other?" Mac asked.

"It was kind of a mutual thing. We only went out a couple of times and that was all the time we needed to know we weren't right for each other," Roger replied. His eyes widened a bit. "Has something happened to Candy?"

"She was murdered."

Mac's words appeared to punch the wind out of Roger. He slammed back against his chair and expelled a huge gasp. "First Melinda and now Candy?" The shock in his eyes was quickly replaced with anger. "Don't think you're going to pin this on me just because I dated them both for a little while. Don't pull some kind of rush-to-judgment crap and arrest me because it might make you look like a hero. If you arrest me, that won't stop the killer…because I'm not the damned killer."

"Calm down, Roger. We're not trying to pin this on anyone. We're just in the gathering-of-facts process in the investigation," Mac replied calmly.

"I've told you all I have to say." Roger stood. "I didn't kill either one of those two woman and I'd like you both to leave now. It's way past my bedtime."

Mac and Callie got up and walked to the front door, which Roger yanked open. "If I have more questions for you and you don't want me to speak to you here, then I'll be glad to take you into the office and do it properly," Mac said firmly.

Roger flushed and drew a deep breath, then released it slowly. "That's not necessary. I'll be glad to cooperate in any way I can. You just really shocked me with the news about Candy."

"We'll be in touch," Mac replied and then he and Callie headed for his car.

"It's too late to do any more investigating tonight," Mac said when they were back in his car. "God, I wish there was a bar we could go to and get a drink," he said.

"I wouldn't mind a drink myself," Callie replied. "But you and I sitting in the Red-Tailed Rooster with two women dead would be a very bad look."

The Red-Tailed Rooster was the only bar in town. It was not only a popular place for the hard-core drinkers, but with its large dance floor it was also a popular place for couples to hang out.

"I agree, but nobody can give us a side-eye if we have a drink at my place. Are you up for it or do you want me to take you straight home?" he asked.

"Sure, I'm up for a drink at your place," she replied. She was pleased with his offer and eager to see what Mac surrounded himself with in his personal space.

They rode in silence until they reached the apartment building where Mac lived. They got out and she followed him to the door of his place. He unlocked the door, reached in to turn on a light and then gestured her inside.

The living room was small and held no personal warmth or appeal. There was a gray sofa and chair, a coffee table and television and that was it. There was certainly no sign of Christmas, no photos of family hanging on the wall, nothing to indicate that anyone lived here. To Callie the whole space felt sterile and more than a little sad.

However, there was one clue for her to recognize and know this was Mac's place. The scent of him lingered in the air. It was the scent of minty soap and shaving cream and the familiar woodsy cologne of his. The combination of those smells always made Callie feel safe and oddly comforted.

He led her into his small kitchen, where once again there was no sign of real life except for the single-serve coffee maker and a toaster on the countertop.

"Have a seat," he said and gestured her to the island, which offered two black-and-chrome bar stools. She pulled one out and sat and watched as he grabbed two glasses from the cabinet and then began pulling several bottles of booze out from a lower cabinet.

"I've got gin, whisky and Scotch and I think there might be a bottle of cinnamon schnapps here somewhere," he said. "What's your poison?"

"Do you have a cola?" she asked and he nodded. "Then I'll take that with a splash of whiskey."

"Coming right up." He fixed her drink and then fixed himself a Scotch and soda. He pulled the bar stool around the island so they faced each other.

"Cheers," he said and they clinked glasses.

They each took a drink and for a moment sat in silence. She felt the weight of both the seriousness of what they were up against and the long day they'd just had tugging at her with weariness. She knew he had to be feeling the same way.

He finally broke the silence with a weary sigh. "What in the hell is happening in my town, Callie?"

"I wish I knew," she replied.

"We've got to find this perp before…" He paused as Callie held up her hand.

"Don't even say it out loud." She knew he was about to say they had to find the perp before another murder occurred. The last thing she wanted to believe was that another victim would show up. "Hopefully this is the end of it. Whatever the murderer wanted by killing Melinda and Candy, he got it and that will be the end of it."

"It won't be over until we have him behind bars," Mac replied. He took another sip of his Scotch and then continued. "I can't believe we've had two horrible murders in just three days."

For the next few minutes, they talked about the crimes and compared the way the two women were left to be found. Aside from the difference that Melinda had a bird in her mouth and Candy had a bird in each hand, the victims were virtually the same.

"What do you think about our latest interview with Roger?" he asked.

"I was surprised that he displayed a bit of anger with us. He's still on the top of my suspect list. Even though he acted shocked by Candy's murder I have a feeling Roger can summon up any emotion at any time if it serves his best interest."

"He definitely seems to like you. Would you ever be interested in going out with him?" Mac stared at her intently.

She nearly choked on her drink. "Are you kidding? The answer would not only be no, but hell no."

Mac nodded. "I figured that would be your answer. So, I don't even know… Are you dating somebody else right now?"

"No, since I moved back here, I haven't found anyone I've been interested in dating," she replied and then mentally added, *except you*. "What about you? Why aren't you dating or married to some nice woman? There are certainly plenty of single women in town who would love to be dating you."

"I haven't really been interested in dating since my divorce. I have no plans to ever get married again, so why would I date?"

She gazed at him in surprise. "You're divorced? I didn't even know you'd been married."

"Yeah, I married Amanda Crowley. We

were married for a little over two years, but ultimately it didn't work out."

She had a vague memory of Amanda. She was a dark-haired beauty who had worked at the local women's wear store. In the two years since Callie had been back in town, she hadn't seen Amanda anywhere around town.

"I'm sorry things didn't work out for you," she said. It was the truth. If he'd truly loved his wife and the marriage hadn't worked out, then she was sorry for him. She always wanted love to win. "Is that why you've decided not to ever marry again?"

"Yeah, once was more than enough for me," he replied. He downed the last of his drink in a single swallow. "I'd better get you home. It's late and tomorrow is going to be another long day."

She had a feeling he needed to take her home before he divulged anything more to her about his marriage and divorce. "I'm ready when you are." She slid off the stool and grabbed her coat and purse from where she'd placed them on the sofa as she'd walked in.

She paused at his front door and turned back to face him. "You shouldn't close yourself off to new relationships just because you had a bad one," she said. "Mac, you are too good a guy to spend the rest of your life all alone."

He stood so close to her and his eyes suddenly darkened and flamed with an emotion she'd never seen there before, and it momentarily took her breath away.

And then he leaned down and took her mouth with his. Shivers of both surprise and pleasure swept through her from head to toe. She immediately responded by wrapping an arm around his neck and opening her mouth to him.

She'd imagined Mac kissing her a hundred times in her dreams, but the reality was far better than anything she could have imagined. His lips were hot and hungry and he tasted of sweet desire and warm Scotch as the kiss continued. He pulled her closer and his tongue slid in to dance with hers.

It all lasted far too briefly before he released his hold on her and stepped back with a deep audible gasp. "I'm so sorry, Callie. That should have never happened." He opened his door and walked outside.

She followed close behind him, the cold night air a slap in her face after the heat of his unexpected kiss. They got into the car and for several minutes they rode in silence, although the tension in the car was palpable between them.

He pulled up in front of her house, parked the car and then he turned to look at her. His eyes were dark and unfathomable. He stared at her for a long moment and then released a deep sigh.

"Callie, in the midst of the stress of these murder investigations you could be a very soft spot for me to fall into and I don't want that to happen. But if that happened, which it won't, you have to understand that it wouldn't mean anything for me. I'm sorry I kissed you. I should have never crossed that line with you and it won't happen again. Now, I'll just say good-night."

"Good night, Mac." She got out of the car and then opened the back door to retrieve her coat. "And just so you know… I really, really liked your kiss," she said and then closed the door.

Chapter Six

That kiss. That damnable kiss kept Mac turning and twisting for what was left of the night. He'd had no forewarning that he was going to kiss Callie until he was actually doing it.

She'd just looked so pretty and he felt as if he'd been thinking about kissing her for the past two years. He tried to tell himself that it had been an unpleasant experience, but he was definitely lying to himself.

Kissing Callie had been beyond wonderful. Her lips had been so soft and filled with a sweet, warm invitation. It was definitely something he'd like to do over and over again. But he wouldn't.

He couldn't allow it to happen again. He'd told her the truth when he'd said she would be an easy, soft place for him to fall. With the stress of the murders so heavy on his shoulders it would be easy for him to want a connection that had nothing to do with murder and death.

And she'd told him she'd liked it. Her parting words to him last night had sizzled in his brain throughout the night. Not that it mattered that she'd liked it. That was just a piece of information to further torment him.

It was just after six in the morning and he now sat at his desk in his office with the second autopsy report in front of him. He read it, finding no real surprises. Candy had been stabbed twenty-two times.

Again, it was an overkill that screamed of some kind of personal rage. What had these two young women, who worked as waitresses, done to anyone to warrant such horrendous deaths? Who had hated them so much?

Candy also had the same ligature wounds. Albertson still believed the women had been held by ropes and they had struggled against them hard enough to leave bloody wounds behind. How horrible it must have been for them to be tied down and then stabbed to death.

After reading the report, he wrote out duties for his deputies for the day. Along with their regular work, each of them would be interviewing people and checking out alibis to further the murder investigation.

Mac was grateful that his deputies were all smart people who used their initiative and didn't need babysitting from him. He told them what he needed from them and they did the best they could to deliver for him.

This second murder changed everything. The townspeople would demand answers and he wished he had some. There would now be a pall of fear overlaying the town and he absolutely hated that.

At the very least he needed to call a town meeting to let people know what had happened before rumors and false information made the rounds. At seven, he made a few phone calls to set up the meeting for that evening.

At seven fifteen he got up from his desk to head to the break room for the morning briefing. He had a quick moment to wonder how things would be with Callie today. Would they be awkward? Would she want to talk about what had happened between them the night before? God, he hoped not. He just wanted to forget about the whole kiss thing.

He walked into the break room and, despite his desire to the contrary, his gaze immediately shot to Callie. Her eyes sparkled with their usual enthusiasm and liveliness as she smiled at him.

He couldn't help but return her smile, then he cleared his throat and began the meeting. It didn't take him long to hand out the daily assignments and to tell the deputies to let everyone know that he would be holding a meeting at seven that evening in the town hall.

Once the men had all left, Mac sank down in the chair next to Callie and opened up the notebook he'd carried in with him. "At nine, I want to be at the pet store to question Craig, but before then I thought maybe you could help me write up something for the town meeting tonight."

"Of course," she said and to his immediate discomfort, she moved her chair closer to his. "What exactly is it you need to tell people."

"Obviously I need to tell them that two young women have been murdered. I certainly don't want to go into all the gory details, but I also want to dispel any false rumors that might be making the rounds."

"What about questions? Are you planning on taking questions from everyone?"

Mac frowned. "I'd rather not, but I'm afraid if I don't then everyone will think I'm hiding things and the last thing I want is for the people in this town to think they can't trust me."

"Mac, it's okay to tell a few little white lies in the interest of protecting the investigation," she said. "Besides, if we can anticipate what some of the questions might be then those are the things you address in your report." She placed her hand on the notebook he'd carried in. "Do you mind?"

"Not at all." He pushed the notebook in front of her and handed her his pen.

He watched as she bent her head down and began to write. He steeled himself against the torment of her nearness. If he allowed it, her familiar scent would dizzy him, her body warmth would burn into his brain at the memory of holding her...of kissing her. He consciously refused to acknowledge any of these things. He had two murders to solve and that was where his focus had to be.

Callie wrote for several minutes and then pushed the notebook back in front of him. "Tell me what you think."

He read the three paragraphs she had written. They were a perfect recap of the crimes, minus the information about the birds and the Santa hats, and exactly what he needed to tell everyone in town. "This is great. Thank you," he said.

"Have you thought anything about the fact that both the victims were blondes?" she asked.

"I have," he replied. He was hoping this wasn't the work of some crazed serial killer who would continue to murder until he was caught. He was desperately hoping that who-ever had killed Candy and Melinda had a specific motive to kill those specific women and now was done.

"I'm hoping that's a coincidence and not a pattern," he continued. "However, I intend to warn the women in this town that they need to travel in pairs or groups until we get this killer behind bars."

"And let's hope they take the warning to heart," Callie replied.

They worked several more minutes fine-tuning Mac's speech for the town hall meeting and once he was confident it said everything he needed to tell the people of Rock Ridge, they stood up from the table and got ready to head out to the pet store.

Callie was quiet on the drive and Mac wondered if she was thinking about their kiss. He hoped not. He hoped that kiss was the last thing on her mind. He certainly didn't want to think about it anymore.

"I still believe it's possible that Roger is our man," she said, breaking the silence be-tween them. "There's something not only sleazy about him, but also we know he has a temper. With him dating both Melinda and Candy, I just can't help but believe he's a number-one suspect."

"I'm definitely leaning that way," he replied, grateful that she was thinking about murder instead of their kiss. "I believe both of the women would have felt comfortable getting into Roger's car after their shifts at the café. Because he works alone in his office, his alibi will be that he was at work, but he has nobody to corroborate his alibis."

"It's possible the nasty breakup with Melinda brought out some kind of darkness in Roger. He apparently takes rejection very hard. And even though he said the breakup with Candy was mutual, we can't know that for sure. Maybe, ultimately, she had rejected him, too."

"If it is him, then I hope he hasn't dated anyone else who might have angered him," Mac said as he pulled up in front of Olson's Pet Palace.

"Let's hope we can get a few answers here," she said as they got out of the car.

The moment they opened the door and walked inside the shop they were greeted by barking dogs in cages. There were also kittens in cages along with rabbits, guinea pigs and hamsters in pens on the floor. Large aquariums held a variety of colorful fish, and rows of items made it easy for people to feed and care for whatever pet they bought.

Craig Olson was in his middle fifties. His dark hair was just starting to turn gray and Mac knew he'd been married to his wife, MaryBeth, for years.

He approached them from the back of the store. "Sheriff," he said with a wide smile. He nodded to Callie and then looked at Mac once again. "Have you finally decided you need a dog?"

Mac laughed. "You know better. I don't have time for a dog. I'm rarely home and it wouldn't be fair for an animal. But I do have some questions for you."

"Okay, fire away," Craig replied.

"Do you know anyone in the area who is raising or keeps domestic kinds of birds?" Mac asked.

Craig frowned. "When you say domestic birds, what exactly are you talking about?"

"Specifically, bobtail quails and pigeons." Mac replied.

Craig's frown deepened as he slowly shook his head. "I don't know of anyone raising those kinds of birds. I can't imagine why anyone would. Those aren't species anyone wants to buy and they certainly don't make good pets like a parakeet or a cockatiel."

"That's what we thought, but we figured if anyone knew anything about it, it would be you," Mac said.

"Does this have something to do with the murders?" Craig asked.

"Unfortunately, I can't discuss anything about the ongoing murder investigations, but I'm having a town meeting this evening at seven to answer some questions," Mac said.

"Good to know. MaryBeth and I will definitely be there," Craig replied. "Is there anything else I can do for you? You sure you aren't in the market for a sweet little puppy?"

"No…no, thanks, Craig. Maybe when I'm not the sheriff anymore," Mac replied.

"Ah hell, Mac, you're going to be voted in as sheriff until you're ninety years old," Craig said with a laugh. "Everyone in town loves and admires you."

A few minutes later Mac and Callie were back in the car and headed to the café to continue to interview the staff. "Have you ever thought about getting a dog?" Callie asked.

"Not really. As far as I'm concerned getting a dog is right up there with getting another wife or having any kind of deep relationship with a woman. It's not going to happen." He spoke the words strongly… forcefully.

The moment Callie had told him she liked his kiss, she'd subtly told him she would be open to a relationship with him. He needed to make it clear to her that he would never be anything to her except her coworker.

Or maybe he was reminding himself that Callie was strictly off limits because the more time he spent with her…the more he wanted her.

THE TOWN HALL was packed with people, along with the chairs that had been set up for the evening. The raised stage on one end of the room held only a podium where Mac would give an update to the people who depended on him and his team to keep them safe.

Jimmy had provided coffee for all and Danny from Danny's Donuts had carried in dozens of the treats for people to enjoy. Despite the sober events that had brought them all together, everyone milled about, talking and laughing with each other.

Callie and the other deputies stood against the wall to the left of the stage, ready to support Mac in any way they could. Callie had confidence that Mac would do just fine He was as well prepared for this meeting as he could be.

Still, her stomach tightened with nervous tension as Mayor Alex Broadbent stepped up on the stage and walked toward the podium. The mayor was a short, squat man who wore his self-importance in the jut of his jaw and the loudness of his voice.

He was not a favorite among the people at the sheriff's office. Occasionally he would come in and puff out his chest and complain about things they were or weren't doing and then he'd fly back out to throw his weight around someplace else. He had only been voted in as mayor because nobody else had wanted the job.

"People…people," Alex said and raised his hands for silence. "Please find seats and quiet down so we can get this meeting underway."

It took several minutes for everyone to settle into chairs and then a hushed pall descended over the crowd. "As you know we've all been brought together tonight due to tragic circumstances that have recently taken place in our town. Two innocent lives were stolen away and I know we're all grieving their loss and wondering what our law enforcement is doing about it."

Mayor Alex continued to talk for the next

ten minutes, speaking about improvements he was hoping to make in the town and all the Christmas celebrations that would occur over the next three weeks. "Starting next week our park will be transformed into the North Pole complete with a Santa to talk to the kids."

Callie frowned in distaste. The mayor obviously had no good sense of timing to be talking about the holiday celebrations taking place in the park where a murdered body had been found.

"Get off the stage," a deep voice finally yelled from someplace in the back.

"Yeah, we came to hear Sheriff McKnight," another male voice cried out. Disgruntled murmurs began to get louder.

Alex laughed and held up his hands once again. "Okay…okay. I hear you. Let's bring out Sheriff McKnight to inform us all about the tragic circumstances surrounding two young women's murders and find out what he's doing about it."

Finally, Alex got off the stage and Mac walked to the podium. Callie's heart expanded. He looked so handsome and so confident.

Everyone hushed once again as Mac stepped up to the podium. He began to talk about the murders that had taken place. He explained that each of the women had been stabbed and that they had apparently been kidnapped off the streets hours before their murders.

His voice held compassion for the victims and an underlying confidence that the guilty would be caught. He finished by telling everyone that they had leads they were following, but also asking anyone who might have information about the two murders to please come forward.

He was eloquent and spoke with no notes, indicating he was speaking from his heart. This was what the people in Rock Ridge loved about him. He was such a good man and Callie wanted to make him *her* man.

After he finished talking, he called for questions. There were only a few, and those were easy for him to answer. Once the few questions had been answered, Mac told the women of the town how important it was that they not be on the streets all alone until the killer was caught. "No matter what time of the day or night, don't be out alone until this killer is behind bars," he reiterated.

Once it was all over, Mac came down from the stage and mingled with the people for a few minutes and then he and Callie and the rest of the deputies left the building.

The deputies went back to their duties and

Callie and Mac drove through the hamburger place for a late dinner and then headed back to the station. It was after ten by the time they sat at a table in the break room.

"Murder investigations are definitely bad for the diet," she said as she unwrapped the bacon cheeseburger and then pulled out her large order of fries from the take-out bag. "I've never eaten as much fast food as I have the last five days."

God, had it only been four days since Melinda's body had been found? It felt as if it had been weeks. The two women haunted Callie at night, invading her dreams with their desire for justice. And Callie desperately wanted to give them justice. But right now, despite what Mac had said about leads in his speech, the investigation was pretty much stalled.

"If you weren't investigating this murder and grabbing late-night fast food, what would you cook yourself for dinner?" Mac asked.

Callie popped a fry into her mouth and chased it down with a drink of soda. "Probably an herb-encrusted chicken breast and some steamed broccoli," she replied.

He raised a dark brow. "Sounds like you must be a good cook."

"I do all right. Most of the things I cook

are from recipes my mom made for family meals. What about you? Do you cook?"

His lips turned up into the smile that always shot a rivulet of warmth through her. "As long as the café is open, I'll never go hungry."

She laughed. "That certainly answers my question."

His smile lingered for another moment and then turned into a frown. "When we finish eating, I'd like to go over some things to see if we've missed anything."

"Whatever we need to do," she replied, although she couldn't imagine that they'd missed anything. It felt as if they had spoken to every single person in town, had followed up on the few leads they had and yet were as clueless as they had been following the first murder.

For the next few minutes, they ate in silence. She felt the weight of the long hours weighing on her shoulders, but she would push herself to her very physical and mental limits to help Mac catch this killer.

Once they were finished eating, they opened the notebooks they'd each carried since the night that Melinda's body had been found.

In this respect they had a common work

practice of keeping continuous notes in ordinary notebooks that they referred to often.

Mac thumbed through his pages and then stopped on a particular page. "What I want to do again is go over the places where Melinda's and Candy's lives intertwined. We need to make sure we've crossed all those t's and dotted all the i's and that we haven't missed anything."

She turned to the pages in her notebook where she had detailed that particular information. "The biggest one is that they both dated Roger," she said.

"We also know both of them got their hair and nails done at Wanda's," Mac added, referring to Wanda's Beauty Spa, the one place in town that catered to women and beauty.

"But we spoke to everyone who worked there and everyone indicated they found Melinda and Candy friendly and fun," Callie replied and looked down at her notes once again. She looked back up at Mac. "This is a small town. The two went to the same stores, drank at the same bar and hung out with the same friends. We've all checked everything possible, Mac."

"I know." He released a deep sigh and closed his notebook. "I just want to catch this creep so badly."

"That makes two of us," she agreed. "Maybe the town meeting tonight will prompt somebody to remember something they saw on the nights of the murders. Maybe somebody will come forward with some new information we can use."

He smiled at her. "There you go again with that eternal optimism."

"Sorry if it irritates you. It's just the way I look at things," she replied.

"It doesn't irritate me at all," he replied. "Sometimes I wish I had a little more of that cheerful outlook on life."

She searched his features. "You don't believe in the joy of Christmas and you don't have a cheerful outlook on life. What happened that stole all that away from you, Mac?"

She suspected it had to do with Mac's first marriage. She wanted to know the ins and outs of him, wanted to understand what drove him and made him who he was. She wanted him to trust her with his emotions and thoughts, not just about the murders but also about his life.

He released a deep sigh and leaned back in his chair. He stared down at the tabletop for a long moment and then raised his head and looked at her once again. His eyes were dark and turbulent…the color of thunder-storm clouds.

"Three years ago my wife walked out on me on Christmas Eve," he finally said. "I didn't see it coming and she totally blind-sided me."

"Oh Mac, I'm so sorry," Callie replied. She wanted to touch him, to pull him into her arms and hold him until the pain in his eyes…in his heart…was gone forever.

He shrugged. "It was a long time ago, but it definitely ruined this particular holiday for me forever."

"Mac…" She reached out and grabbed his hands in hers. "I'm so sorry if she hurt you. I can't imagine any woman foolish enough to ever walk away from you, but don't let her steal your joy of Christmas…all the joy of your life…away."

He briefly rubbed his thumbs across the back of her hands and then pulled his away and stood. "I think on that note it's time to call it a night."

She wanted so much more from him. She wanted to know why his wife had left him. Did he still love her? Is that why he had no interest in another relationship? Because he was holding out hope for some kind of a rec-onciliation with Amanda?

She didn't ask any of those questions. As she rose from the table a huge weariness slammed into her. Even though it was almost eleven thirty, the earliest she would be home since Melinda had been murdered.

"Maybe something will happen tomorrow that will bring us clarity concerning this killer," she said once they were in his car and he was driving her home.

"I still don't understand why the birds were left with the bodies," Mac replied. "They have to mean something to the killer. Otherwise why were they left?"

"Maybe Roger killed both of the women for breaking up with him and then he left the birds to throw us off track and make us believe some crazy person killed them."

"Or some crazy person with a vendetta against blonde women really did kill them and unless he somehow messes up, we're never going to catch him," he replied.

"There you go with that negativity again," Callie said half-teasingly.

He flashed her one of his sexy half smiles. "You're right. I need to change some of that about myself."

For the first time she saw the lines that dug deeper down the sides of his face, the ones that fanned out from his tired-looking eyes.

All of the deputies were feeling the long hours and hard work that had come along with these murders.

They were quiet for the rest of the ride. He pulled up at the curb in front of her house, put his car into Park and then turned to look at her.

"I know we're all running on empty right now," he said. "I don't want to see you at the office tomorrow before nine. Take some extra time to sleep in a little. It's obvious this investigation is going to be a marathon and not a sprint and if we continue to work these crazy hours, we're all going to burn out."

"And what time are you coming in tomorrow?" she asked.

"I don't know. I'll know when I get up in the morning."

"You know you need to take care of yourself as well," she replied. "You're working longer hours than anyone."

"Yeah, I know." He flashed her a tired smile. "I'll see you tomorrow after nine."

She wanted to take his hand and pull him out of the car and into her king-size bed. She didn't necessarily want sex or anything from him. She just wanted to somehow take care of him, to make sure he got a good night's sleep and ate a good breakfast in the morning.

There was a part of her that wanted to take care of him, and there was a part of her that wanted to be cared for by him. She now understood why he hated Christmas and why he'd lost faith in love. Apparently, his breakup with his wife had broken his heart... had broken him.

She wanted to change all that, but as she got out of the car and headed toward her front door, she realized that a romance between her and Mac might never happen.

For the first time since she'd started working for Mac, she faced the fact that the girlish crush she'd had on Mac was transforming into a grown-up woman's love. She also had to face the fact that no matter how much she might want him, he might never love her back, he might never be *her* man.

Chapter Seven

For the next two days Mac held meeting after meeting with his deputies. They went over and over the elements of the crimes, searching for anything and everything they might have missed.

He and Callie beat the streets, talking to the same people over and over again, checking and rechecking whatever alibis they could and trying to ignore the fact that they had no clues, no real leads to follow.

Mac had never worked with a partner before. Despite the fact that Callie intrigued him as a man. In spite of how much he'd like to let himself go and fall into the warm depths of her eyes, accept the sweet fire he knew she might offer, he wouldn't do that.

However, he did appreciate her being an intelligent partner both as a sounding board and somebody who threw out ideas of her own. He enjoyed her company, both when they were talking about the murders or when they were just small-talking about anything other than murder.

Once again, he was driving her home. It was ten thirty after another fruitless day. The silence between them in the car wasn't one that made him uncomfortable. Thankfully, Callie wasn't the kind of woman who needed to fill every silence with conversation and he appreciated that about her.

When he pulled up in front of her house, he couldn't help but notice the colorful lights that shone from a Christmas tree just inside the large picture window. They looked cheerful and inviting.

"Nice tree," he said as he parked at the curb.

"Thank you. After a long day of a murder investigation, it's nice to come home to a pretty tree with festive sparkly lights. Maybe you should get one for yourself. You know... embrace the season and all that."

He released a dry laugh and shook his head ruefully. "You're like a mischievous elf constantly whispering in my ear."

She laughed, the deep, sexy sound sweeping through him on pleasant notes. "You can't blame an elf for trying."

Mac's phone rang, jarring their conversation. He answered on speaker. The caller identification showed that it was Deputy Cameron Royal. "Cameron, what's going on?" Mac asked.

"Sheriff…we've got another one."

Cameron's words sliced through Mac, and Callie grabbed his forearm as if to keep them both grounded. "Where?" Mac asked.

"It's Linda Bailey and she's in front of the bank," Cameron replied.

"We'll be there in five." Mac hung up and threw the car into Drive. He got back on the phone and called in more deputies and the medical examiner.

"Linda Bailey…she's another blonde," Callie said softly when Mac got off the phone. In Mac's peripheral vision he saw her reach up and touch one of her own blond curls.

Mac's stomach clenched tight and a faint nausea rose up inside him as he thought of Callie in the hands of this madman. She would definitely be the blond-haired young woman who might draw the killer's attention.

Still, right now all he could think about was that there was yet another innocent woman who had been killed.

What in the hell was happening? He was the sheriff in this town and yet he felt as if he'd been dropped into the middle of a horror film where he didn't know the plot and couldn't see the end. He was terrified for his town.

Once again, he was thankful that it was another cold, blustery night and late enough that nobody else was on the streets. However, that didn't take away the sickness inside him.

There was only one bank in town and Linda Bailey worked as a teller there. She was a pretty blonde and Mac would guess her to be in her late twenties or early thirties.

He saw Cameron's car parked at the curb and he pulled in just behind it. Together he and Callie got out of the car, pulled on gloves and booties and then approached the scene.

As with the other two women, Linda's body was posed with a little Santa hat on her head. She had no coat and she was clad in a long-sleeved white blouse and black slacks. The blouse was bloody in several places with what Mac assumed was the result of knife wounds.

At her feet were three dead chickens.

Mac stared at the dead birds and myriad emotions filled his head. Confusion about what the birds meant, horror that another woman had met her death at the hands of a madman and the whisper of self-doubt that had haunted him since his ex-wife had left him.

Are you good enough? The words fluttered in his head and made all the muscles in his body tense. His ex-wife certainly hadn't thought so. The answer was obviously no. Linda made the third woman who had been killed. How many more women would have to die before he could get the perp behind bars?

More deputies arrived and they began to process the scene. As Mac worked along with everyone else, he had no time to entertain any more self-doubts. Maybe this one would yield the clues he needed. Perhaps Linda's death wouldn't be completely in vain and this was the case that would solve all the murders.

Maybe some of Callie's optimism was actually rubbing off on him. He glanced over to where she was talking to Deputy Johnny Matthews. She looked earnest and he appeared…appeared smitten.

A strange emotion swept through Mac. Jealousy? Ridiculous, he scoffed to himself. "Mac, we're ready to take the body," Richard Albertson said as he stepped up next to Mac. "I don't expect any real surprises when I do the autopsy. I'm sure it will pretty much be like the last two."

"Unfortunately, I'm sure you're right," Mac replied.

"Have you figured out anything about the birds?"

Mac frowned. "Right now we don't have a damned clue as to what they mean and why they're being left at the scenes. I think if we could solve that much, we'd be well on our way to making an arrest."

"I hope that happens soon," Richard said.

"That makes two of us," Mac replied.

It took another two hours after Linda's body had been carried away to finish up processing the scene. Linda lived alone in an apartment in the same complex as Mac. Her parents had moved out of Rock Ridge to Kansas City. He would wait until morning to call them, a call he dreaded making.

It was one thirty when he and Callie got to Linda's apartment to have a look around and see if she'd left any clues as to what had happened to her. There had been no phone found with her body, but Mac was hoping to find out what carrier she used for cell service and request records from them. He was still waiting for records from the other two victims.

"Sorry to wake you at this time of the

morning," Mac said to Ed Canton, who was the apartment building manager.

"Sorry for the circumstances," Ed replied. "Linda was a good tenant, always paid her rent on time and never caused any problems." He unlocked the apartment door and shoved it open. "If you don't mind, just lock up after you're done."

"Will do," Mac replied.

He and Callie stepped into the apartment and Mac flipped on an overhead light. The living room was attractively decorated with a beige sofa and chair and throw pillows in a bright yellow.

On one wall was a desk holding a computer. Mac immediately went there to see if there was anything on her social media that might be helpful. While he was working with that, Callie disappeared into what he assumed was the bedroom.

Mac did a cursory search on all the social platforms and it didn't take him long to learn that Linda wasn't much of a poster. He was grateful to find a password book in her desk drawer. With that in hand, he closed down the computer and began to pack it up to take with them.

Deputy Pete Taylor was their computer expert. He knew computers inside and out.

If there was anything on Linda's computer that might lead them to her killer, then Pete would find it.

He turned as Callie came out of the bedroom. "Find anything interesting?" he asked.

"Nothing, except for the fact that Nathan must be doing some work for her in her closet. It looks like some new shelves have been added and more are ready to be put in."

He finished wrapping up the computer cord. "How do you know that Nathan is doing the work?"

"There's a wooden toolbox in there with Nathan's name carved into the side of it," she replied. "What about you? Anything on her computer?"

"I just did a quick search of her social networking and didn't see anything worthwhile. She also had a couple of texts from several friends that I looked at but they were all about a week old. At first glance I would say she wasn't into the whole social networking thing, but we'll see what Pete can find."

"Sounds good," Callie replied.

They finished searching the apartment and then left the building. "There really isn't much more we can do tonight," Mac said wearily as he drove to take Callie home.

"First thing tomorrow we'll head to the bank to start questioning people."

"And we need to establish a time line as to what she did and where she went yesterday. So far it seems like he takes his victims and holds them for at least six hours or so and then he kills them," Callie replied.

"If Linda worked yesterday then he broke the pattern," Mac replied. "If she didn't get off work until five, then he only held her a couple of hours before killing her." Mac clenched his hands on the steering wheel. Who was this creep and when was he going to make a mistake? "Obviously we also need to speak to Nathan again."

"Maybe this will be the one," Callie said softly. He could hear the weariness in her voice. "Maybe this will be the one that breaks the case wide open."

"If it doesn't, it might be time for me to call in the FBI," Mac replied. "It's obvious now this person is looking and acting like a serial killer and we have no real clues as to his identity."

He hated the idea of admitting defeat, and that was what a call to the Feds meant. It would mean that he and his team couldn't do it, that they didn't have the capacity to solve the crime.

But despite that it would look like defeat to his team…to his town…he also wanted the killing to stop. If it took the FBI to make that happen, then he would be all in. He pulled up in front of Callie's house and turned to tell her goodbye.

Her eyes blazed with a surprising energy in the dashboard light. "Mac, don't do anything rash. Don't give up on your team yet," she said fervently. "Don't give up on yourself just yet."

"Callie, I have to be honest with myself. Three women are dead and we don't have a lead—we don't even have a single clue to find the killer. Maybe the FBI has more tools than we have. All I care about is getting this killer behind bars before another woman dies. If it takes the FBI to do that, then so be it."

"At least wait until we examine all the evidence in Linda's murder. Who knows where the investigation will lead us," she replied. "Mac, you're the smartest man I know. All you need is one little clue, one little break, and you'll catch this killer."

His heart warmed at her words. "Callie, I appreciate the vote of confidence. We'll see what happens in the next couple of days or so."

As he'd done every night since this nightmare had begun, he watched her walk to her front door. And once again the lights from the tree in the window winked and twinkled cheerfully. When she disappeared into her house, he drove home.

Once inside his apartment, despite the lateness of the hour, he was too wired up to immediately go to bed. He sank down on his sofa and his mind filled with the images of the three dead young women and the birds that had been found with each one of them.

The birds had to be at the center of the case. But damned if Mac could figure out how. What did the birds mean to the killer? Was it some kind of a ritualistic kind of thing? He needed to check with surrounding towns to see if they had seen something like this.

He was also concerned because the killer was on such a fast track. He was scarcely giving them time to investigate one murder before another one was committed. What had triggered the killings in the first place?

He released a deep sigh, leaned his head back and closed his eyes. For the first time he wondered what it would be like to come home to Callie's place.

He knew it would be warm and welcoming…like Callie herself. He imagined it would smell like peppermint and cinnamon and vanilla from the candles she burned.

The lights on her tree would create a soft ambience that would inspire peace and tranquility. God, he wished he was there with her right now.

Instead, he was in his cold, sterile apartment and headed into all the dark places in his mind as he dreamed of the murder victims night after night.

Chapter Eight

By eight o'clock the next morning Mac was seated at a desk in the bank interviewing one of the bank tellers and Callie was seated at a desk across the room interviewing another one of the tellers.

Barb Timmons was an attractive brunette in her middle thirties. She openly wept at the news of Linda's murder. "I just can't believe this," she cried and grabbed several tissues from the box on the desk. "She was such a sweet person." She dabbed at her eyes.

Callie gave her a few moments to gather herself together. "When was the last time you saw or spoke to her?"

"Yesterday was her day off, so it would have been when the bank closed on the day before. She and I didn't really hang out so we didn't talk on the phone or text each other unless it had to do with bank business."

"And why was that? Why didn't the two of you hang out?" Callie asked.

"We were just at different places in our lives. I'm married and have a small child at home and Linda is…was…still in the single lifestyle, so we didn't hang out after-hours."

"The last time you talked to her did she mention going out with anyone? Do you know if she was dating anyone specific?"

"She didn't mention anything, and I'm pretty sure she wasn't dating any one person." Barb shook her head ruefully. "I do know she was excited about Nathan Brighton doing some work in her closet. He was installing some shelves and she told me she couldn't wait to put her shoe collection there instead of spread out all over the floor."

"So, you have no idea what she might have planned for her day off?" Callie asked.

Barb shook her head and tears once again filled her eyes. "I… I just can't even believe she's gone. I can't imagine anyone wanting to hurt her."

"If you think of anything, anything at all, would you please give me or Sheriff McKnight a call?" Callie removed one of Mac's cards from her shirt pocket and handed it to Barb.

"I promise I'll let you know if I think of anything," Barb replied.

"Thank you for your time and now you can get back to your regular work." Callie watched as Barb made her way across the bank lobby to her position behind the counter as a teller.

Callie glanced over to Mac, who was now interviewing the bank manager. There was nobody else for Callie to speak with, so she remained seated at the desk waiting patiently for Mac to finish up.

During the last couple of days of her and Mac working together for such long hours, they had shared pieces of their lives with each other.

She now knew he liked his burgers without tomatoes, his steak rare and his eggs over easy. She'd also learned that he liked old rock and roll music, that his favorite season was spring and that when he was stressed out, he rubbed the back of his neck.

He'd told her that like her, he'd had an idyllic childhood. His father worked for the Rock Ridge Fire Department and his mother had been a stay-at-home mom. A year before, his father had retired and he and his wife had bought a small farm about forty-five minutes away. Although he and his parents were close, he'd confessed that he had yet to visit them on their new farm.

She'd talked to him about Lily, the sister she had lost, and had shared stories about when the two were young. He'd been warmly supportive as he'd listened to her talk about her sister and she'd felt as if their friendship had grown deeper with all the conversations they'd shared.

The schoolgirl crush she'd had on him was truly blossoming into something deeper and more grown-up. She was on the verge of being completely and totally in love with him.

And with that love came worry. It was the worry of a woman for her man. What concerned her about him right now was his decision to potentially call in the FBI.

Mac's entire self-identity was that as sheriff of the town he loved. If he wound up calling in the Feds, it would be an admission that he no longer believed in his team…and more importantly that he no longer believed in himself. And if that role as a trusted, confident sheriff was taken away from him, then what would he be?

As she saw Mac stand and hand the bank manager his card, Callie also got up and met him at the front door. Together they walked out of the building and into another cold, blustery day.

"Anything?" Mac asked once they were in the confines of his car.

"Only that Linda was excited about the shelves Nathan was building into her closet. Nobody I spoke to had any idea about what she might have done yesterday on her day off."

"The only information I got was that Linda was a good employee, always on time and never a problem. But nothing about her day-off activities or about anyone who might want to hurt her."

"So, what next?" she asked.

"We talk to Nathan again."

Nathan wasn't at home, but they found him at the café. He sat in a booth alone and offered them both a friendly smile when they approached him.

"Hey, Nathan. Mind if we join you?" Mac asked.

"No, not at all," Nathan replied.

Callie scooted in on the bench seat facing Nathan and Mac slid in next to her. Almost immediately waitress Nancy Weatherby appeared. "Morning Callie… Sheriff," she greeted them. "What can I get for you this morning?"

"Just coffee for me," Mac replied.

"Make that two," Callie added.

"Two coffees," she replied. "Nathan, you doing okay?"

"I'm fine as a fiddle," Nathan replied. "You two should have ordered the pancakes," he said once Nancy had left the booth. "I always get the pancakes because they're so good." As if to prove his point, Nathan took a big forkful of the fluffy cakes.

"We both ate breakfast earlier," Mac said. They made small talk until Nancy brought the coffee and then left the booth again.

"I understand you've been doing a little work for Linda Bailey," Mac said and then took a drink of his coffee.

"Yeah, I've been building some shelves in her closet for her." Nathan wiped his mouth on a napkin and then frowned. "But I think maybe I did something to make her mad at me and maybe she doesn't want me to do the work for her anymore."

"What makes you think that?" Mac asked. Callie took a sip of her coffee and kept her gaze on Nathan.

"Yesterday morning I was supposed to show up at her place to keep working on the shelves, but when I got there I knocked and I knocked and she never came to the door. I tried to call her a couple of times yesterday but I kept getting her voice mail. Then I stopped by there again this morning and she still didn't answer the door, so I figured I'd done something to make her mad even though I don't know what it was." Nathan shook his head and cut into his pancake.

"She wasn't mad at you, Nathan. At some point yesterday Linda was kidnapped and murdered," Mac said.

Nathan gasped, his eyes opened wide and he slowly lowered his fork back to his plate. "For real? Sh-she's dead?"

Mac nodded. "She's really dead. We found her body last night."

"But who would want to hurt her? She was a really nice lady," Nathan replied. "She was really nice and patient to me. Why would somebody even want to…to kill her?"

"That's what we're trying to figure out," Mac replied. "Did you see anything suspicious around her place when you went there yesterday morning?"

Nathan slowly shook his head. "I didn't, but I wasn't really looking for nothing. I'm sorry." His big, round eyes welled up. "I should have been looking around."

"There's nothing to be sorry about," Mac assured him. "But if you think of anything please call me." Mac withdrew one of his cards and slid it across the table. "I'll also make arrangements with a deputy to get your tools to you sometime later this morning."

"I appreciate that. I can't do much without my toolbox," Nathan replied. "And I guess I need to look for a new job."

Mac stood. "Somebody will be in touch with you about your box. Thanks for your time, Nathan."

Callie slid out of the booth and together they left the café. "I think we'll head back to the office and see what Tim found in the evidence that was gathered last night around the body," Mac said. Deputy Tim Franklin was their evidence guy. Mac made a quick call to make sure Tim would be there to meet with them.

Knowing how busy the big labs were and the time waiting for results was often months, four years ago Mac had sent Tim to school to learn all about gathering and analyzing evidence. Much of their work could now be done with their little local lab while still using the big labs for deeper analyzation and toxicology results.

"So, what did you think about Nathan?" Mac pulled out of the bank parking lot.

"He seemed genuinely surprised when you told him about Linda. I'll say one thing—he would have to be the stupidest killer in the world to kidnap and kill a woman and then leave his toolbox behind for law enforcement to find it."

"I agree."

She watched his fingers whiten as he gripped the steering wheel tightly. "Mac, you need to relax a bit. Otherwise, you're going to have a heart attack before this is over and this little Christmas elf doesn't want to see that happen to you."

His fingers immediately loosened on the wheel and he flashed her a quick smile. "I've never had my own personal Christmas elf before. Shouldn't you be at the North Pole making toys or something?"

"There are elves that make toys and then there are elves who spread joy and happiness. I'm one of the latter," she replied with a grin of her own.

The levity between them only lasted a few minutes, halting the moment he parked in his space behind the sheriff's office. They went in the back door, took off their coats and then met Tim in the small room that held equipment to display photos and a metal table to view evidence more closely.

Callie knew the official evidence room was in the basement and held years' worth of items from crimes that had occurred long before Mac had become sheriff.

Tim was a serious man in his mid-thirties. He was tall and thin and wore thick horn-rimmed glasses that did little to hide the sharp intelligence in his brown eyes.

"What have you got for us, Tim?" Mac asked as he and Callie sat in the two chairs the room held.

Tim shut off the overhead lights and cast a photo onto the viewing screen. "As you can see there is a lot of dirt and several cigarette butts that were gathered in the area where Linda's body was found. I don't believe the cigarettes were left by the perpetrator. They're too old to have been left last night."

"I can't imagine our man setting the body on the bank steps, putting a Santa hat on her head and the birds at her feet and then hanging around to smoke a cigarette," Callie said.

"What else?" Mac asked of Tim.

Tim pulled up another photo of more dirt and something small that was shiny and bright. "What you're looking at here is a fourth of a carat cubic zirconia that probably fell out of a piece of jewelry…possibly a ring or a necklace. It could have fallen out of something last night or it could have been there for weeks. Unfortunately, there's no way of telling."

"Anything else we should know about?" Mac asked.

Tim turned the lights back on. "Nothing."

"Where is he?" A deep voice thundered down the hallway. "I know he's here somewhere. I saw his car parked out back."

Callie recognized the voice… Mayor Broadbent.

"Thanks, Tim," Mac said and left the room. Callie hurried after him. Mayor Broadbent stalked down the hallway and met Mac.

"Sheriff, I need to talk to you right now," Alex said. "I need to know what in the hell you're doing about these murders. Every time I turn around there's another body. I need answers that I can take to the people of this town. Young women are scared to go out of their houses."

"What do you want me to say, Alex? My men and I are out there trying to find answers. We're working long hours and doing the very best we can. I held the town meeting and told everyone in town what was going on," Mac countered.

"Well, your best isn't good enough. I'm holding another town meeting and I need something to say that will help ease the fear,"

Alex replied. "For God's sake, man. Give me something."

"Right now is probably not the time for you to try to ease the fears of the young women in this town. They need to be afraid, there's a killer out there who is targeting young women and right now we don't know who the killer is."

Mac reached up and rubbed the back of his neck in obvious frustration. "We're doing everything we can but if I were you I'd be damned careful about what you say to alleviate the healthy fear that each young woman in this town should be functioning with right now."

Alex's eyes flashed darkly. "Don't tell me how to do my job, Sheriff, especially when you don't seem to be doing yours so well these days."

Callie watched as every muscle in Mac's body tensed. "Is there anything else you have to say to me?"

"If these murders continue to happen, maybe it means you aren't really up for the job. I wouldn't be surprised if somebody didn't start a recall effort to get somebody else in position who can do the job properly."

"Thanks for the heads-up, and I really appreciate your support. Now, you're wasting my time and I have murders to solve. So, if you'll excuse me. Callie, let's head back to the evidence room."

Callie turned on her heels and headed back down the hallway the way they had come. She was acutely aware of Mac hot on her heels. Definitely hot—she could feel his anger radiating out from him.

Tim was no longer in the room. Mac flipped on the light and once Callie was inside, he slammed the door behind her. This was the first time she'd seen Mac really angry.

His eyes blazed and his lips pressed together in a thin slash. He paced the small confines of the room a couple of times and then stopped and drew in a deep, audible breath.

"He's a total jerk, Mac," Callie blurted out. "And most of the people in this town can't stand him. He's nothing but a pompous ass and you shouldn't pay any attention to him or what he says."

Mac drew another deep breath and a small smile curved his lips. "Thank you…you took the words right out of my mouth. He is a pompous ass." The smile lasted only a moment and then he frowned. "But the longer these murders keep happening, the more the people will demand answers and right now we still don't have any. I'm failing the people of this town."

"We'll get him, Mac." She walked over to him and placed a hand on his forearm. "Nobody in this town has lost faith in you. The people love you and realize you're working as hard as you can to solve these murders."

She stood so close to him she could smell the scent of his shaving cream and his cologne. She could feel his body heat warming her from head to toe. The muscles beneath her hand slowly lost some of the tension.

The blaze in his eyes transformed into something different than anger and her breath caught in her throat. Was he going to kiss her again? Oh, she hoped so. She'd thought about their last kiss for what felt like forever and she desperately wanted another kiss from him.

He dipped his head toward her, his lips coming within mere inches of her own, and then he suddenly stood straight up and stepped back from her. "We need to get back to work. Let's hit the road."

Callie nearly moaned in disappointment. She'd wanted the kiss she believed he'd been about to give her. However, she wanted to catch this killer before he killed another woman...before he destroyed Mac.

FOR THE NEXT four days Mac and Callie stalked the streets, looking for answers. They had been unable to learn anything about Linda's movements on the day of her death, leading Mac to believe that she had been taken fairly early right from her apartment and before Nathan had knocked on her door. If that was the case, because there had been no indication of a break-in, then Linda had known her killer and had opened the door to him.

In all three cases, Mac believed the victims had known and had trusted their killer. So, who in town warranted that kind of trust? That kind of respect? If he could just figure out that common denominator...

It was now after ten and he was driving Callie home after another long, fruitless day. "Have you considered that our man still might be Roger?" Callie asked, breaking the silence that had lingered between them as he drove.

"Isn't it possible that maybe he killed Linda to throw us off? He killed Melinda and Candy because they rebuffed him. Since those two murders pointed a finger directly at him, maybe he killed Linda and hoped that would take the heat off him."

"At this point nobody is off the suspect list as far as I'm concerned," Mac said. His phone suddenly rang. He stared at it for a long moment. Phone calls at this time of night were never good, especially since he saw it was one of his deputies who was on duty calling.

Mac knew even as he answered the call. There was another one. This time she'd been left in front of the hardware store just off Main Street.

"Dammit," he exclaimed as he hung up the phone.

Callie remained silent as he turned his car around and headed to the scene. He couldn't speak at the moment and he was grateful that she didn't talk, as well.

The last four days had had him hoping that the killer was done. And now…another victim. Dear God, who was behind these murders? What had triggered this killing spree? What did the birds mean? The same questions whirled around and around in his head, questions that had begun with the first murder. And now the count was four dead women and the same questions hadn't been answered.

He felt sick in his very soul. The people in this town depended on him to provide law and order, to protect them so they could sleep easily at night knowing that he and his men were on the job.

He made the call to get everyone to the scene and within minutes he and Callie arrived at the hardware store. Rhonda Hickson was against the door, a Santa hat on her head and four ordinary blackbirds at her feet.

"What's with these damned birds?" Deputy Adam Cook asked as Mac and Callie approached where he stood on the sidewalk.

"I wish we knew," Mac said with a frown. He looked at the body. It was like he was having a déjà vu moment. The face had changed, but the scene was the same.

Rhonda was an attractive blonde in her mid-twenties. She worked as a night nurse at the small Rock Ridge hospital and now she was dead, her white blouse stained with her own blood.

Blackbirds and chickens, pigeons and a quail… What did they all mean? How was Mac supposed to make sense of nonsense? What did the birds mean to the killer? And dammit, why couldn't Mac or anyone else figure it out?

As they all worked to process the scene, he

thought maybe Callie was feeling the same way he was—defeated and lost in a miasma of dark emotions.

He looked over at where she stood out of the way of the medical examiner. She was quieter than he'd ever seen her. She wasn't asking questions, she wasn't making comments, but she just stood, looking as bleak as he felt.

Their eyes locked and hers instantly warmed as they held his gaze. For just a moment he didn't want to think about murders and birds. He didn't want to smell the scent of blood and death.

He wanted this murderer behind bars but at the moment what he really wanted to do was fall into the warmth of Callie, to lose himself in her evocative scent. He wanted to get out of his own head and be in hers, where maybe he wouldn't feel the weight of the murders so heavy on his shoulders for a little while. He wanted to drive her to his place, take her to bed and make love to her. He just wanted to escape into her for a few mindless moments.

With a frustrated sigh, he broke off eye contact with her and instead watched as Rhonda's body was bagged and taken away. By the time the crime scene was completely processed, it was almost two in the morning. Rhonda lived at home with her parents and Mac dreaded another notification of a beloved one's death. But it had to be done now. The last thing Mac wanted was for them to find out about their daughter's death from somebody else.

Despite the lateness of the hour, Callie insisted she go with him to make the notification. It was as difficult as the last three. He delivered devastation with empty platitudes. He gave them utter heartbreak with apologies he knew did nothing to ease their pain.

By asking questions he learned that Rhonda wasn't dating anyone in particular and only had a few good friends from the hospital with whom she socialized.

He and Callie were silent for several minutes as he drove her home. He was grateful for the quiet. He was in a place where he had no words left as his brain whirled with what he needed to do next in order to investigate this most recent murder.

If he didn't find a credible lead or a clue to point to the killer within the next two days, then he was going to admit defeat and call in the FBI. He had to…before another murder occurred.

He pulled up to the curb in front of Callie's house. Instead of getting out of the car, she turned to look at him. "Mac, maybe this will be the one that…"

He held up a hand. "Callie, stop. I don't want to hear any of your cheerleading right now."

He must have spoken more sharply than he intended, for the light in her eyes doused and instead tears filled her eyes. She looked as if he'd stabbed her to her core. "Then I'll just say good-night and I'll see you in the morning," she said.

Before she could slide out of the car, Mac took hold of her arm and held her in place. "I'm sorry, Callie. I didn't mean to hurt you." He released a deep sigh. "I'm just processing so many things in my head right now and we both know we're in trouble. This killer is flying under our radar and murdering women at an incredible pace. The only clue we have is a small cubic zirconia diamond that may or may not have fallen out of a ring or a bracelet, a diamond that may or may not have even come from the killer."

He stopped only because he was too exhausted to continue. He dropped his hand from her arm and rubbed the back of his neck where a bundle of muscles tensed painfully with stress.

"I think maybe both of us need to get some

sleep," she said softly. She smiled at him, a bright, beautiful smile that momentarily lit up the darkness in his heart. "Good night, Mac. Tomorrow will be a better day." With that she slid out of the car, grabbed her coat and then headed to her door.

Mac pulled away from the curb and hoped she was right. Tomorrow *had* to be a better day. Maybe this really would be the one that would yield the clues he needed to make an arrest.

For the next three days Mac and Callie and the rest of the deputies worked almost around the clock to find a connection between the victims other than their blond hair. They interviewed all of Rhonda's coworkers and friends from the hospital in an attempt to find somebody who might have a grudge against her.

They learned that Ben Kincaid had been in the area of the hardware store an hour or two before the body had been left. In talking to them, he'd told them he'd bought a new bird feeder so the birds could eat throughout the snowfall. He also spoke again of an evil spirit that walked the streets of the town.

All the deputies and Mac exchanged ideas about the birds but had yet to come up with anything that made any sense.

Each morning Mac thought about calling in the Feds, but he was hoping for something to finally come together before he made the call. There were eleven more days until Christmas and he was hoping to give his town the gift of a killer behind bars.

He had done another town meeting, once again warning all women in the town to stay in pairs or a group whenever they were out and about. Thankfully, the mayor had stayed off his back since their last encounter. The last thing Mac needed was Broadbent to put any more pressure on him than Mac was already putting on himself.

As he took Callie home on the evening of the third day after Rhonda's murder, he was worried about his "partner." Her eyes appeared less bright than usual and she seemed to have slowed in putting one foot in front of the other. It was obvious the ridiculously long hours they'd been working had finally gotten to her.

"I want you to take tomorrow off," he said to her as they arrived at her place.

She looked at him in surprise. "What are you talking about? We're in the middle of an investigation."

"You definitely need a day off," he replied.

"But…but what are you going to do without me?" Her blue eyes searched his features quizzically.

He smiled at her. "Callie, I'll do just fine without you for a day. Now go, get to bed and I don't want to see you anywhere near the office tomorrow."

"Are you sure?" She released a slow sigh that sounded like utter exhaustion.

"Positive. You need a day off, Callie," he said firmly.

It was only while he was driving home that he recognized not only did Callie need a day off, but he needed a day off from Callie.

Despite all the stress of the murders, he was aware that his emotions where Callie was concerned were beginning to get out of his control. He looked forward to seeing her each morning and he hated dropping her off at her house each night.

She was definitely getting under his skin like no other woman before her had. He didn't even remember feeling like this when he'd first started dating his ex-wife.

Callie was the kind of intelligent woman he'd always imagined himself with for the long haul. There was no question he thought she could be his soft place to fall. And he also knew she cared about him.

He felt that caring each time she touched

him and he yearned for her touch far more than he should. In fact, he was falling in love with the beautiful blonde whose smiles warmed his heart and who continued to sneak in bits of Christmas into the office. His little Christmas elf was working some magic.

He didn't want to be in love with Callie. He didn't want to be in love with anyone. After his first marriage he told himself he would never trust a woman again. More than anything right now he wanted to catch a killer and more than anything right now he had to figure out how to not fall any deeper in love with Callie.

Chapter Nine

It was a little after ten o'clock when Callie opened her eyes to the midmorning sun filtering in through her bedroom curtains. She started to jump out of bed, but then remembered and instead snuggled deeper beneath the blankets and released a small sigh.

As much as she hated to admit it, she'd needed the day off.

The long hours had drained her and she'd definitely needed the extra sleep and time to recharge. The past two days she'd been so tired she'd felt as if she were walking through sludge. Not only was her body completely exhausted, but her mind was, as well.

She felt as if she'd been thinking about murder forever. She knew Mac intended to call in the FBI in the morning if nothing broke today. He'd given them all the last couple of days to come up with something…anything…

that would move the investigation forward. And they'd all failed him.

The birds left at each murder scene haunted her dreams. If they could only figure out what they meant. They were obviously part of the killer's ritual and meant something important to him.

At least now the women in town had taken Mac's warning to heart. As soon as the darkness of night fell, the streets emptied of people. During the day if women were out and about, they were always with a friend or in a group. They all were taking their safety very seriously and hopefully making it impossible for the killer to take another victim.

That was the only reason Mac had put off calling in the FBI. However, Callie knew tomorrow morning he was probably going to make that call. Hopefully the FBI with their more sophisticated tools would be able to crack the case.

No more thoughts about murder today, she chided herself. It was her day off and she intended to spend it doing things that made her happy.

With that thought in mind, she finally pulled herself out of bed and headed for a shower. Forty-five minutes later she sat at her kitchen table with a cup of coffee and a piece of toast. She finished off the toast and then as she drank the rest of her coffee, she made a list of the people she wanted to buy Christmas presents for.

Normally by this time of the month she'd already be finished with her shopping and the presents would be wrapped and ready to go. But normally she wasn't involved in a murder investigation.

She always bought gifts for the other dispatchers and she also had a few friends she usually bought for. But she hadn't had much to do with her friends lately. She also wanted to find something really special to give to Mac.

Mac. Her heart expanded with thoughts of him. There was no question she was falling deeper and deeper in love with him even though she wasn't sure how he felt about her. There were times she thought she saw love for her shining from his beautiful gray eyes, and then there were other times when she felt as if he intentionally shut her out.

She finished up her list, determined that she wasn't going to think too deeply about anything today, and then got up. She rinsed her cup, tucked her list into her purse and then put on her coat.

By the time she got outside, the early-morning sun had given way to a steel-colored sky that portended snow. She hadn't watched any weather forecasts lately, but she definitely smelled snow in the air.

She smiled. There was nothing she loved more than a white Christmas and if it snowed now and the temperatures remained below freezing then she'd get her wish.

Her smile immediately fell away. Her first hope was that by Christmas the killer would be behind bars and the fear that had possessed the small town would finally be gone.

She walked briskly down the sidewalk, grateful that her home was walking distance from the downtown area. The first place she intended to go was Janie's Stuff and Things, a quaint little shop that carried a little bit of everything beautiful, fun and unique and was owned by one of her good friends.

She hoped nobody got offended seeing her out and about today doing shopping in the middle of the murder investigation. Surely most of the people would realize that everyone deserved a day off. Besides, Janie was one of the friends Callie had loved to hang out with before her life changed with the murders.

She entered the shop and the scents of peppermint and evergreen and sugar cookies greeted her. It was the heady scents of Christmas and that instantly filled her with the joy of the season and with the desire to shop for special presents for special people.

"Hey, Callie," Janie greeted her from behind the cash register counter. "Or should I say Deputy Stevens?" Janie added teasingly.

"Oh, stop," Callie replied with a laugh. Janie walked around the counter and the two women hugged.

"I know you've been working practically day and night. What, did Sheriff McKnight finally give you some time off knowing that he was working you to death?"

"He's not working me to death. These murders are. I have today off, but tomorrow I'll be back at work as usual."

"So, how is it working with him?" Janie asked curiously.

Callie instantly felt a blush warm her cheeks and before she could say anything Janie grinned and winked. "Ah, so it's like that," she said. "Tell me the truth—have you slept with him yet?"

"No," Callie replied firmly, the heat in her cheeks growing hotter. "And why would you even ask me something like that?"

"Because I know you've always had a mad

crush on him and you're two single consent-ing adults, so why not?"

"We've had a few more-pressing things on our minds lately," Callie replied. "But I don't even want to think about that right now. I'm here to shop."

"Good, you know I'm always willing to take your money," Janie replied with a laugh. "I'll just let you get to it. Let me know if I can help you with anything."

"Thanks, Janie. I'm just going to wander for a little while and look at all the treasures." And there were lots of treasures.

She found pretty little trinket boxes with pink jeweled, old-fashioned telephones on top and placed one for each of the dispatch-ers into her little shopping basket.

As she walked around the store, she felt herself relaxing like she hadn't in the past few weeks. Seeing all the unique and fun things the store offered, along with the cheer-ful Christmas music playing overhead, fed her soul.

She found most of the presents she needed but unfortunately found nothing right to buy for Mac. What did you buy for a man who seemed to want for nothing, a man who had no hobbies and was a workaholic?

From Janie's she stopped into the coffee

shop and had a mug of hot chocolate with whipped cream. She sat at a window seat and people-watched as she enjoyed the hot drink.

She now couldn't imagine why she'd ever wanted to move away from this small town. Her parents had teased her and said she'd eventually tire of the big city and want to come home. She wished she had come home sooner. She wished it hadn't been their deaths that had brought her back.

And she desperately missed her younger sister. Lily had been three years younger than Callie. She'd been the typical pesky little sister, but despite her peskiness, the two had been very close. And now she was gone forever, thanks to a drunk driver. Callie shoved these sad thoughts away.

It was after four when she finally returned to her house. It had been a successful shopping day even though she hadn't found a gift for Mac.

As she made herself dinner, big fluffy snowflakes began to fall outside the windows. She ate and watched them fall, glad that she was inside the warm confines of her home for the night.

After eating a bowl of soup and a salad for dinner, she went upstairs and changed out of her jeans and blouse and into a soft fleece jogging suit. She went back downstairs and into the living room. She turned on some Christmas music and then sat on the floor next to the sparkling tree to wrap the presents she had bought.

Several times throughout the day she'd thought about calling Mac to see how things were going, but she'd decided not to. Surely he would have called her if anything with the case had broken loose and she didn't want to bother him by contacting him.

Once the presents were all wrapped, she built a fire in the fireplace, made herself a cup of hot cocoa and then curled up beneath a soft blanket on the sofa.

Holiday music continued to play as she stared into the flames that danced in the fireplace. Once again thoughts of her parents and the sister she had lost intruded into her head.

She had so many happy Christmas memories with them and as she sipped her hot drink, she allowed those remembrances to play freely through her mind.

Tears filled her eyes and she swiped at them angrily. She had sworn to herself that she wouldn't grieve for them, but rather she would celebrate them.

As memories of her family slowly ebbed away, thoughts of murder filled her head.

She hoped the killer was behind bars by Christmas. She wanted to celebrate the holiday with no thoughts of murder in her brain. And she wanted Mac to be free of the stress and weight this killer had placed on his shoulders.

She finished her drink and then leaned back and closed her eyes and let the music wash over her. She had definitely needed today to refresh and recharge. She was now eager to get back to work tomorrow. And she was definitely eager to see Mac.

She was just about to get up and head to bed when one particular Christmas song played. Her eyes snapped open and her heart began to beat a rhythm of excitement. Was it possible?

Could it be an answer to some of their questions about the murderer? She threw off her blanket and hurried up the stairs to where her computer was on a desk in her bedroom.

For the next half an hour she did some research and jotted down her findings in her notebook. When she was sure of what she had, she called Mac.

He answered on the first ring and she didn't even give him a chance to greet her. "Mac, can you come over to my place right now?"

"Callie, it's almost ten o'clock and there's

two inches of snow on the ground. What's going on?"

"I don't want to go into it over the phone. Please come here… It's important. I swear you won't be sorry."

"This better be good," he replied and then with a muttered goodbye, he hung up.

Immediately doubts began to fill Callie's mind. Was it good? Had she found a clue to the case or was she only deluding herself? Could she be wrong? She grabbed her notebook and headed back downstairs. She desperately hoped she was right because if she was, it would be the first thing that made sense in this whole horrendous case.

AFTER HEARING THE forecast for six to eight inches of snow, Mac had been in contact with all his deputies. Tonight they were all on traffic duty. There were always the fools who thought they could drive through the snow, fools who found themselves stranded on the side of the road or crashed into another vehicle. If they got eight inches of snow the whole city would shut down and the only vehicles moving would be the snowplows.

The last thing he needed was to be heading to Callie's house, but there had been a simmering excitement in her voice that definitely had him curious.

He was so used to having her around almost every minute of every day and he hated to admit that he'd missed her presence next to him today. In fact, it bothered him that he'd missed her as much as he had.

It made him want to gain more distance from her. And yet here he was in the middle of a stalled murder investigation on a snowy night rushing to her home.

When he pulled up in front of her house, the lights from the tree sparkled outward and reflected beautifully on the new fallen snow. Even though he was curious as to why she had called him here, he was reluctant to go inside because he knew he might like being in her space.

He pulled up in her driveway and parked and wondered again why she'd called him here. "Only way to find out is to go inside," he muttered to himself.

He got out of the car and approached the front door. The snow was coming down even faster now. Before he could knock on the door, she opened it. "Mac, come on in." She opened the door wide enough for him to step inside.

She looked beautiful and comfortable in a

soft pink hoodie and matching jogging pants. She led him from the foyer into a large living room. A fire snapped and popped in the fireplace and everywhere he looked there were Christmas decorations. It was exactly the way he'd imagined it to be…exuding warmth and invitation. He shrugged out of his winter coat and laid it on the top of the beige overstuffed sofa.

"So, why am I here?" he asked.

"Please, have a seat." Her eyes sparkled with what appeared to be excitement as she gestured him to the sofa. She joined him there, sitting so close to him he could feel her body heat.

"Are you going to tell me why I'm here?" he asked.

"Absolutely. I think I've figured something out about the murders. Mac, it's not about the birds."

"What do you mean?"

"We've been trying to figure out what the birds meant and we've believed the murders were somehow about the birds. Now I don't believe the birds mean anything other than a manifestation of trauma."

"I don't understand. What's changed your mind?" Mac looked at her quizzically.

"'The Twelve Days of Christmas'… Do

you know the song?" she asked, that shine of excitement still in her eyes.

He frowned. "Not really… Isn't it something about five golden rings?"

"Before you get to the golden rings there are colly birds and French hens, turtle doves and a partridge in a pear tree," she replied.

She reached out and took both of his hands in hers. "Four colly birds… They are blackbirds, Mac. I looked it up. Three French hens…three chickens. Then there's two turtle doves, which was two pigeons, and finally a partridge, which is like a big quail. The murders are not about the birds, Mac. They're about Christmas. Somehow, I believe thoughts of Christmas triggered our killer. Somebody out there hates Christmas as much as you do and that's how we'll find him. He's following the song."

Mac tried to digest what she'd just said. Was it possible she was right? Was it possible the birds weren't what was driving the murders, but rather it might be something traumatic that had happened at Christmastime that had triggered the killer?

An edge of excitement danced through him and he squeezed her hands. "Maybe this is the break we've been waiting for."

"It's definitely a new path to investigate,"

she replied. "We're really going to find him now, Mac." To his surprise she leaned forward and wrapped her arms around his neck. "I swear we're going to get the bastard," she whispered into his ear.

He needed to distance himself from her. He couldn't think when she was so close to him and yet even as he processed that thought his arms enveloped her.

She'd brought him a new lead to follow, but it was getting late on a snowy night and there was really nothing that could be done tonight about it.

He loosened his arms from around her as she reared back from him. He thought she intended to move completely out of his arms, but she stopped moving backward and suddenly her lips were right in front of his.

"Mac." She said his name softly and with what sounded like a deep yearning.

"Yeah?" he replied, just as softly.

"Are you going to kiss me?" Her eyes were sparkling blue pools that he could drown in.

"I might." A white-hot desire seared through him, a desire he'd been fighting against since last time he had kissed her.

"When will you know if you're going to?" Her tongue made a quick dash across her upper lip as if in anticipation.

That single evocative action broke him. "I know right now," he murmured just before his mouth took hers.

It wasn't a soft, tender kiss; rather it was something hot and wild as their tongues immediately swirled together. She tasted faintly of chocolate and a fiery desire.

Her arms tightened around his neck as she leaned into him. Her full breasts pressed against his chest and, despite the danger alarms that rang in the back of his head, his arms encircled her and pulled her even closer against him.

The kiss seemed to last forever and yet didn't begin to satisfy the ravenous hunger in his soul for her. He ended the kiss only to slide his lips down her slender neck. He felt half-dizzy with his desire for this woman... for Callie...and he consciously refused to listen to any more alarms that went off in his head.

"Mac," she whispered softly and once again he thought he heard a deep yearning for him in her voice. She leaned back just enough for her fingers to go to the top button of his shirt.

He sucked in a deep breath as her gaze held his. Blue fire...and he felt himself falling mindlessly into her flames. She unbuttoned his first button and then leaned forward to kiss the bare skin she'd uncovered. Another button…another kiss. More buttons unfastened until she could push his shirt off his shoulders.

She unfastened his gun belt and took it off and laid it on the sofa next to them. She then leaned back from him and pulled her hoodie over her head, exposing a pretty pink bra and full breasts he definitely wanted to touch. She stood and reached out a hand to him.

Someplace in the back of his mind he knew if he took her hand wonderful things would happen…things he would probably regret. But right now, regrets were the last thing on his mind.

He was lost in Callie, lost in her scent, her warmth and the sweet essence of her very bright soul. He placed his hand in hers. She pulled him off the sofa and led him to the throw rug in front of the fire.

He pulled her into his arms, loving the feel of her bare skin against his. Their lips once again met in a searing kiss that rivaled the heat cast out from the fireplace.

When the kiss ended, she sank down to the rug and pulled him down along beside her. "Mac, I want you to make love to me," she said, her voice low and sexy.

All thoughts of anything else fled his mind. His blood surged through his veins and his want…his need…for her was the only thing in his head. Still, he tried to maintain some semblance of himself.

"Callie." He reached up and gently pushed one of her curls away from her face. "I've told you I don't want a relationship."

"I just need to know, do you want me?" Her gaze held his intently. "Do you want to make love with me right now in this moment, Mac?"

"There's nothing else I want to do more right now," he replied honestly.

She smiled at him, that beautiful smile that toasted his insides even more than they already were. "Then what are you waiting for?"

He gathered her into his arms once again and as they kissed, his hands stroked up and down her back and then finally stopped at her bra fastener. Her heartbeat mirrored his own, fast and frantic. In his haste to unhook her bra, his fingers became clumsy.

After a moment or two of fumbling, she reached behind her and unhooked it. She shrugged it off her shoulders and suddenly he was holding her warm, full breasts in his hands. Her nipples were pebbled into hard peaks and as he ran his thumbs across them, she moaned.

His lips followed his hands. He licked and sucked as she writhed beneath him, torching his desire even higher. Her fingers clutched at his shoulders as she continued to moan with her pleasure.

She suddenly rolled away from him. In one graceful movement she took off her pants, leaving her in a wispy pair of black panties.

"Now you," she said half-breathlessly.

He didn't hesitate. He first took off his shoes and socks and then shucked his khaki slacks, leaving him clad only in his black boxers.

The flickering light from the fire loved her features, painting them in a soft golden glow. He gathered her into his arms once again and it wasn't long before her panties and his boxers went the way of their other clothing.

He held her against him, her bare skin warm and inviting against his own. She shifted to his side and once again his tongue teased the tip of her breasts at the same time his hand caressed down her hip.

He was fully aroused and ached with his need, but before he let himself go, he wanted to give her as much pleasure as possible. As his hand moved toward her very center, she rolled over on her back and parted her legs to welcome the intimate touch.

As he dipped his head to taste her lips once again, his fingers danced over her moist and heated skin. She moaned once again and rose up to meet his touch. He quickened his pace as she reached down and grabbed his hard length. He pushed her hand away, afraid that he would lose it too soon.

And then she was there. He felt the shudders that raced through her as she cried out his name over and over again. She fell back against the rug, panting as her eyes gleamed with gratification. That gratification lasted only a moment and then she reached down to encircle his shaft once again. "Take me, Mac. I want to feel you inside me."

Her words nearly broke him. He moved on top of her and hovered there, momentarily staring deeply into her eyes. The blue depths bewitched him, shining not just with sexual eagerness, but something deeper and even more captivating.

Slowly he entered her, groaning with the exquisite pleasure that instantly overtook him. Her warmth surrounded him tightly and immediately he began to stroke in and out of her. She gripped hold of his buttocks, urging him to move faster and faster.

He complied and felt himself quickly reaching his climax. Thankfully before he did, she moaned, her muscles all tightened and then with a shuddery sigh she melted.

That was all it took for him to reach his limit. His climax exploded from him, quaking through him with a force that left him weak and boneless.

When it was finished, he collapsed alongside of her, waiting for his panting breaths to return to normal. Beside him, Callie was breathing unusually fast and seemed to be waiting for her normal to return, as well.

She finally rolled over to face him and placed her hand on his chest. "You are so beautiful, Mac," she said in a half whisper.

He smiled at her. "Thanks, but the real beauty in this room is you." He tried not to focus on the regrets that were already forming in the back of his head. He ran a hand through her soft blond curls and released a deep sigh. "I probably need to get up and get out of here."

"Why don't we get up from here and go upstairs to my bed." She cuddled closer against him. "It's probably still snowing outside, Mac. There's nothing more you can do tonight. Spend the rest of the night here with me."

Oh, it was so tempting. She was so damned tempting. Gracefully she got to her feet and once again she held out her hand to him. And once again he knew that if he took her hand he'd be breaking all the promises he'd initially made to himself where she was concerned.

Still, he took her hand and stood. In for a penny…in for a pound, he thought. Besides she was right; there was nothing he could do about the investigation tonight. She put on her panties and he pulled on his boxers and grabbed his gun from the sofa and then together they went upstairs.

Her bed was covered in a peach-colored spread with matching accent pillows. Floral pictures hung on the wall. The top of the dresser held bottles of perfumes and an earring stand.

The room looked feminine, but also as equally warm and welcoming as the living room had been. "There's a bathroom right here," she said and pointed to a doorway in the bedroom. "And there's another one right down the hallway."

"I'll head to that one," he said.

Once in the bathroom he washed himself off and then pulled his boxers back on and stared at his reflection in the mirror over the sink. "What are you doing, man?" he asked his reflection. But the man in the mirror had no answer.

There was a window over the tub and he leaned over to get a peek outside. There appeared to be about four inches of snow on the ground and it was still coming down. It was not a night for man or beast to be out and about.

Besides, the thought of sleeping next to Callie, instead of him sleeping in his bed all alone, warmed his heart in a way it hadn't been warmed in a very long time. And that scared him more than a little bit.

Maybe it was time he remind her that in the long run none of this meant anything to him, that this night was an outlier and something that would never happen again.

Still, it was difficult to hold on to that thought when he walked into the bedroom and saw her sitting in the bed and clad in a pink, sexy little top.

She smiled and patted the other side of the bed. "In, Sheriff McKnight. I know how much you need to get some good sleep."

He got into the bed…the soft bed that seemed to envelop him. He released a deep sigh as his aching bones and muscles relaxed into the mattress. It was only when he was completely relaxed that she leaned over and gave him a tender kiss on his cheek.

"Sweet dreams, Mac." She then turned and shut off the light on her nightstand, plunging the room into darkness.

"Good night, Callie," he replied. He decided he needed to have a talk with her in the morning and explain to her that this had all been a mistake. Even with this weighing heavy on his mind, and the fact that the investigation had suddenly taken a new twist, he was asleep within minutes.

Chapter Ten

Callie awakened spooned against Mac's body. His arm was slung around her as if to keep her in place and snuggled tight against his big, warm body. She knew he was still soundly asleep because he snored lightly.

She didn't want to awaken him and in any case she wasn't inclined to move. She wanted to revel in his body warmth and in the familiar smell of him. Their love-making the night before had been everything she'd dreamed about.

He'd been a tender, yet commanding lover. He'd made sure she found her release before he allowed himself his own, which made him a generous lover.

Surely last night meant something to him. He had to have feelings for her, feelings that were bigger than mere lust. She had no doubts about her feelings toward him. She was in love with him. She wanted to wake up every morning in his arms. She didn't want to be his deputy; she wanted to be his life partner.

His snoring halted and his body tensed, letting her know he was awake. She found herself tensing up, wondering how he was going to handle the morning after.

He pulled his arm from around her and rolled away. "Good morning," he said as he sat up.

She turned over to gaze at him. "Back at you. Did you sleep well?" He looked so hot in her bed with his bare chest golden in the early-morning light that drifted through her window.

"I can't remember when I slept so well," he replied. He threw off the blankets and stood. "But duty calls and I need to get to the office." He walked over to the window and peered out.

"How does it look out there," she asked, although she was more interested in the view inside. He was clad only in his boxers, and she couldn't help but admire his physique. His shoulders were so broad and his stomach and hips were slim. His legs were long and muscled. He took her breath away all over again.

"A bit nasty," he replied. "Looks like we

got about four and a half or five inches of snow." He turned back to face her. "Thank God you live on Main Street, which I'm sure by now has been cleared off."

She sat up. "Let me fix you some breakfast before you head in to the office."

"I appreciate the offer, but I need to get out of here. Don't get up on my account. I'll just head downstairs and get out of your hair. I'll relock your door when I leave."

Before she could say anything else, he walked out of the room. Minutes later she heard her front door open and then close. She flopped back on the bed and released a deep sigh.

Now she knew how he intended to deal with the morning after. He didn't intend to deal with it at all. He'd basically pretended that nothing had happened between them the night before.

She glanced at the clock on her nightstand. It was a few minutes after seven. At least he got a good night's sleep, she thought as she sat back up and got out of bed.

She padded into the bathroom and got into the shower. As the water beat down on her, she continued to think about Mac. Even knowing how he'd acted this morning she wouldn't take back a single minute of their time together.

If nothing else ever happened between them she would have the memory of making love with Mac forever etched in her heart, in her very soul.

With the loss of her family, maybe she was trying too hard to fill the loneliness in her life. Maybe she had to realize that where Mac was concerned, she was chasing a dream that would never come true.

She turned off the shower water, got out and dried off and then dressed in her uniform. As she strapped her gun around her waist, she shoved Mac out of her mind. Instead, she turned her thoughts to the murders they had to solve.

If she was right, and she truly believed she was, the next murder would have some form of five golden rings left at the scene. However, with this new information she was hoping they could catch the killer before he acted again.

With this thought in mind, she ran down the stairs, pulled on snow boots and her coat and then left her house to walk to work. It was Sunday morning and with a lack of people on the streets and the new fallen snow, there was an unusual hush. Her boots crunched the snow beneath her feet, providing the only sound in the air.

As she drew closer to the back door of the sheriff's office, her thoughts turned to Mac once again. At some point in the day would he talk to her about what had happened between them last night?

If he didn't, she had to maintain her professionalism. Their personal life was one thing, but they had a killer to catch and with the new information they had new paths to investigate. That's where her focus needed to be.

When she walked into the break room nobody else was there. She hung up her coat and then went down the hallway to Mac's office. She knew he was there because his car was parked out back.

She knocked and heard him say for her to come in. She opened the door. He was seated at his desk, paperwork before him and a deep frown across his forehead.

"Good morning again," she said and sank down in the chair facing his desk.

"Yeah, good morning," he replied.

"What has that deep frown on your face?"

"If these killings are happening because something traumatic happened to our killer at Christmastime, then I'm trying to figure out how we investigate that."

"Maybe the first thing we need to do is revisit the people on our suspect list and see if they've done anything to decorate for Christmas. If the perp hates the holiday, then surely he wouldn't do anything to celebrate it."

"Despite all of our investigating we only have the same suspects that we had with the first murder." His frown grew deeper. "We've got Roger, who had reason to get revenge against two of the victims. Then there's Ben, who was seen in the area right before two of the bodies showed up."

"And Nathan, who was on Main Street when the first body showed up and then was working for Linda Bailey, who was another victim," she added.

"Aside from those three, no other suspects have come to the surface," Mac replied.

"So, we focus our energy on those three. We recheck their alibis for the times of the murders. We go hard at them and either find our man if he's one of the three, or we completely get them off our suspect list."

He nodded. "I studied the lyrics of 'The Twelve Days of Christmas.' We now know the next thing is five golden rings. When the stores open today, we need to see if we can find out who might carry cheap golden rings."

"Mac, I truly believe we're on the right track now," she said.

For the first time since she'd walked through his office door he smiled. "I do, too. All we have to do now is wait for the stores to open. Between it being Sunday and all the snow, they won't open for another couple of hours. In the meantime, we can probably catch all our suspects at home this morning."

Callie stood and returned his smile. "Then come on, partner. Let's get going."

He stood and grabbed his coat from the back of his chair. Together they walked down the hallway. He paused just outside the break room while she grabbed her coat and then she followed him out the door and to his car.

"We now have four time lines of the murders and when the victims were posed on the street, so we need to check alibis for all four of the times," Mac said the minute they were in the car.

It was obvious he had no intention of addressing what had happened between them the night before. He apparently intended to pretend it had never happened.

He got on his radio and contacted Glen Malick, who was in charge of the road crews.

He arranged for Glen to clear the roads to Nathan's and Ben's places. Like Callie, Roger lived on Main Street and so the road to his place was already plowed and salted. They headed there first.

"As I recall Roger had a Christmas tree up when we talked to him the last time," Callie said. "What we need to find out is what he really thinks of Christmas."

He flashed her a quick glance. "I'll leave it up to you to delve into lover boy's mind. I'll stick to grilling him about the alibis."

"Gee, thanks," she replied drily. "I have a feeling being in Roger's head for too long would make me want to throw up."

Mac laughed, the warm sound breaking some of the tension she'd felt wafting from him since they'd awakened together that morning.

Thankfully, the road crews had done their job, making it relatively easy to get to Roger's house. "You two again?" Roger said the moment he answered Mac's knock. "What now?" He glared at Mac with unabashed anger.

"Can we come in or are you going to have us conduct our business on your front porch?" Mac asked.

Roger stepped back from the door, allowing them to enter. "Wow, what a beautiful tree," Callie exclaimed as she walked over to the tree that sparkled with multicolored lights and held glittery miniature ornaments in the shapes of dogs and cats clad in Santa suits.

"Thanks," Roger said, his tone warming up a bit.

Callie turned back around and smiled at him. "You must love Christmas to have such a wonderful tree."

"Christmas is okay. Honestly, though, I put up the tree and all the trimmings because it's all kind of a chick magnet." He winked at her. "If I get a woman in here, the Christmas stuff shows I have a sensitive side."

Roger's "sensitive" side wasn't showing minutes later as Mac grilled him about his alibis for the days and nights of the murders. Rather he became angry and hostile.

"How in the hell am I supposed to remember exactly where I was on all those dates?" Roger asked emphatically. "I can tell you where I wasn't. I wasn't anywhere near the victims. I didn't kill those women. I've never killed anyone in my entire life."

Callie believed him. There was a passion in his eyes that spoke of truth telling. Besides, surely the guilty party would have their alibis ready for the asking.

Roger might be smarmy and without much

of a moral compass when it came to women, but she didn't believe he was their killer.

Mac finished up the questioning. "You guys are killing my love life," Roger said as he walked with them to the door. "Every woman in town is steering clear of me now because you keep questioning me about these murders."

"The good news is I think we're done with you for now," Mac replied. He apparently felt as she did, that Roger wasn't their man.

He confirmed that once they were back in the car. "Initially I thought he was our best suspect, but now I'm just not feeling it," he said.

"I agree. Roger might be many things, but I don't believe he's a killer."

"So, we'll pop into Ben's next. Hopefully by now the road crews have cleared the roads to his place."

They rode in silence. She could smell his cologne in the small confines. It was a scent that had made her feel safe and protected throughout last night. She wished he'd say something about what they had shared the night before, but if he didn't want to talk about it, then she didn't want to make him uncomfortable by bringing it up.

Her relationship, or lack thereof, with Mac

flew from her mind as they pulled up outside Ben's house. Ben was clad in all-black winter gear and was up in one of the trees. As Mac and Callie got out of the car, Ben pointed a rifle at them.

WHAT THE HELL? Mac froze and desperately hoped Callie had done the same. His hand itched to get his own gun out of the holster, but he was afraid the movement might make Ben shoot him.

The air snapped with a dangerous energy. "Ben, what's going on this morning?" Mac yelled.

"Evil walks the earth," Ben shouted back. The barrel of his rifle pointed first at Mac and then at Callie. "I have to be on guard to keep the evil away from me and my home."

"Ben, you know me. I'm not evil…and neither is Deputy Stevens," Mac replied. "Why don't you come down from there so we can have a little chat."

The gunshot exploded, sending birds flying from all the other trees in the area. The bullet whizzed by Mac's ear. Mac immediately crouched down and motioned for Callie to do the same. "I don't want to have a chat," Ben yelled.

Mac's heart beat a thousand times a minute

as his blood rushed to his head. He'd never seen Ben so fired up before. At the moment he was both unpredictable and dangerous.

Right now, Mac had reason to arrest the man. He'd shot at a sheriff and that was against the law. But first he had to somehow get Ben out of the tree and disarmed.

He also wanted to protect Callie and the only way to do that was to make himself the bigger target. Tentatively he rose up once again, holding his breath to see if Ben would fire on him again.

"Ben, tell me what I can do to help you," Mac stated.

"Nothing can help me. The bad spirits have me in their sights."

For the first time Mac wondered if Ben was on some kind of medication...some medicine that he'd perhaps stopped taking. It appeared he was having some kind of a psychotic break. Had he killed the women while in the clutches of some form of madness?

"I can help you fight the bad spirits, Ben. If you come down and talk to me, we can fight the spirits together."

Ben was quiet for several long moments. "What do you know about fighting bad spirits? You're normal—you probably don't see the shadow people that are all around me, just waiting to suck the life out of me."

"You're right, Ben. I can't see the shadow people, but that doesn't mean I can't help you. Come down so we can talk and I can tell you in more detail how I can help you."

Mac held his breath, waiting to see what the man would do. Ben once again pointed his rifle in the direction of Callie. "What about her?" he yelled down.

"I can promise you that she is a good spirit. She's full of light and love and hope and all things beautiful. She can help make the bad spirits go away. Trust me, Ben. She can help, too."

The three of them remained frozen in place for several tense moments and then, finally Ben began to make his way down the tree.

"Can I have the rifle?" Mac asked once Ben was on the ground.

Ben caressed the rifle's stock and his green eyes gazed intently into Mac's. "This is a special rifle that kills bad spirits."

"If you give it to me, I promise I'll take good care of it," Mac replied. He was aware of Callie standing up on the opposite side of the car.

Ben continued to hold Mac's gaze and Mac

held his breath. Finally, Ben handed the rifle to him. "Callie, can you come here so Ben knows you're his friend, too?" Mac's voice was even and calm.

Callie joined them, and smiled at Ben. "Hi, Ben. Remember we met before? Deputy Stevens is kind of a mouthful, so you can call me Callie."

Mac was grateful that she appeared soft and warm and friendly. It was just what was warranted for the situation.

He felt the tension waft from Ben as the man stared into Callie's smiling eyes. "Do you mind if Callie holds your special rifle?" Mac asked.

Ben tensed once again and adrenaline shot through Mac. He had no idea if Ben would cooperate or not. At this point he didn't even know if Ben had another gun on him. Ben gave a curt nod and Mac handed the rifle to Callie.

"Ben, I'm afraid I'm going to have to arrest you now," Mac said. He reached for Ben's arm, but Ben twirled away from him and took off running.

"Dammit," Mac muttered as he raced after Ben. He cursed himself for speaking out loud what he'd intended to do. He'd figured if he could get Ben held down at the jail for the

next twenty-four hours, they could either figure out if he was the killer or if he simply
needed medical attention.

Ben maneuvered around the trees like a
slithering snake, dodging easily the feeders
and wind chimes and other strange items that
hung from the trees while Mac cursed and
bumped into the hanging things as he worked
to keep Ben in his sight.

He feared what might happen if Ben managed to slip away from him. Obviously, Ben
was suffering a great amount of paranoia.
Mac worried about what that paranoia might
make Ben do. Had it made him kill four innocent women?

Despite his snow boots, Mac slid down
to one knee and then hurried back up again.
His breaths came in deep pants, the cold air
aching in his lungs.

Suddenly a figure jumped out at Ben and
took his legs out from under him. Callie. She'd
apparently come from another direction and
got just in front of Ben to take him down.

Before Ben could get to his feet, Mac
reached him and grabbed him at the same
time he pulled out his handcuffs. "Thanks,
partner," he said to Callie, who had gotten to
her feet and now held her gun pointed at Ben.
"No problem," she replied and smiled that

beautiful smile that always lit up something inside him.

Ben had begun to sob as Mac got him into the cuffs. "Ben, it's going to be okay," Mac said as gently as he could. "We're going to take good care of you."

Callie holstered her gun and then placed a hand on Ben's shaking shoulder. "Ben, bad spirits can't get into our jail. In fact, they can't even enter the sheriff's office at all."

He looked at her with tear-filled eyes. "Are you lying to me? Is…is that really true?"

"It's true," she replied. "You'll be safe in jail until we can get your home safe for you to come back again."

Ben held her gaze and then slowly nodded. "Okay."

Mac did a quick pat down of Ben and discovered a large knife in one of Ben's pockets. "That's special," Ben explained. "It kills bad spirits that come around me."

Mac placed the knife in an evidence bag. Once again, his heart beat a little quicker. Was it possible the knife was the murder weapon? It appeared clean, but if it had been used to stab the four women to death, then hopefully the lab would find any trace of blood that sealed the deal.

Ben remained docile as they got him into

the back of the patrol car and then checked into jail. Throughout the ride Callie continued to talk to Ben in calm, soothing tones. Mac admired the fact that she'd read the situation correctly and was acting accordingly. Once Ben was in jail, they returned to the car.

"Damn, I forgot to check to see if Ben's front door was locked," Mac said. "He specifically asked us if we'd make sure it was locked. We need to go back and make sure the door isn't unlocked."

"What are you going to charge him with?" Callie asked.

"If he isn't our killer, then I probably won't charge him with anything," Mac replied. "I can hold him for up to twenty-four hours before I either have to charge him or cut him loose." He glanced over to her and then back on the road. "That gives us twenty-four hours to catch this killer."

"Great, just what we need…more pressure," she replied drily.

"Keep in mind, we don't have a search warrant. However, I do intend to go inside and see if I can find some medication or the name of a doctor who might be able to see Ben while we have him in custody."

"He definitely needs some help," she agreed. "Nobody should be that afraid."

"He's always been strange, but this is something different than strange. I think he's had some sort of a psychotic snap."

"Do you think we found the murder weapon?" she asked.

"If that knife stabbed those women, then the case is solved. I don't think it's out of the question that Ben might have seen the women as bad spirits and attacked them. But we don't stop investigating until we know for sure that Ben is our man."

When they got back to Ben's, sure enough his front door was unlocked. Callie remained at the front door while Mac went inside to check for any medication he might find.

The first thing he noted was there was no sign of Christmas anywhere in the place. He made his way through the living room and into the bathroom. A peek in the medicine cabinet yielded several bottles of medicine. Mac pocketed the bottles and then walked into the bedroom.

Unlike the living room with its odd statues and wall hangings, this room was pretty sterile, just holding a twin bed, a dresser and a nightstand. There was nothing hanging on the walls and there were heavy black curtains covering the single window.

On the nightstand Mac found two more bottles of medication and pocketed them, as well. As he walked back to the front door, he gazed all around him. Nowhere did he see a sign that four women had been killed here.

Still, he couldn't discount Ben's current mental state. He still believed it was possible the man saw the women as evil spirits and so he'd killed them. Ben had plenty of land around his house where he could have taken the women and stabbed them to death.

"No sign of Christmas in there," he told Callie as he got back in the car. "But I have a pocketful of medicine bottles that need to be sorted out. We'll head back to the office and I'll see if I can make contact with the prescribing doctor. Once that's done, I'll call Nathan and see if he'll meet us at his home."

Minutes later Mac was in his office and on the phone to a Dr. Tony Georgino, who was the doctor on all the prescription bottles. Mac explained Ben's behavior and the doctor immediately believed Ben was off the medication he was prescribed for anxiety and schizoaffective illness.

When Mac told him Ben was a suspect in the murder of four young women, the doctor immediately came to Ben's defense. "I have been treating Ben for the past six years. In my professional opinion Ben doesn't have a homicidal bone in his body. However, if it would help, I could drive in and see Ben sometime late this afternoon."

"That would be great," Mac replied. "Maybe you can give me some insight that I need."

They made arrangements for the doctor to meet Mac at the office at four o'clock. Mac hung up the phone but remained seated at his desk.

He only had a little bit of circumstantial evidence with his three top suspects. Beyond that there was no evidence to point to anyone else. Roger had fallen off their suspect list, leaving Ben and Nathan at the top.

His head filled with all the details of each and every murder. They had spent so much time spinning their wheels about the birds. Now he believed the murders had to do with Christmas. The bodies had been posed with Santa hats on their heads and an enactment of "The Twelve Days of Christmas."

As he thought of Ben firing the rifle at him, he couldn't help but wonder if Dr. Georgino might be wrong. Maybe the doctor didn't know about how much his patient might have deteriorated. Maybe he didn't realize that throughout the last couple of months Ben's obsession with who he perceived was evil had turned deadly.

Then his thoughts moved from murder to Callie. She'd surprised him, both with her takedown of Ben, and then in her display of utter compassion for the man. She had to have known the knife they'd found on Ben made it even more likely he was their killer and yet she had been soft and gentle with him.

He was in love with her. In another lifetime he would have asked her to be his wife and he would have been incredibly happy to be planning a future with her.

However, his fear was greater than his love. He'd known his ex-wife, Amanda, since grade school. When he'd married her, he'd believed she was a good woman with a compassionate and giving heart. But ultimately, she'd shocked him with her utter ruthlessness. She'd not only walked out on him, but she'd also gutted him in the process.

How was he to know Callie wasn't the same? How could he trust that things would be different with her? Sure, Callie might have a crush on him now, especially after him making love to her the night before, but ultimately he would bore her or disappoint her and things would crumble and turn ugly between them.

He'd taken a chance on love and marriage once, but it didn't matter how much he cared about Callie; he just wasn't willing to do it again.

Last night he'd given her a false signal. By making love to her, by then sleeping with her in his arms, he'd definitely given her the wrong impression. He was sure he'd given her the signal that he was all in on having a relationship with her. And before this night was over he needed to let her know that wasn't the case.

Chapter Eleven

Mac was silent as they drove to Nathan's place. Callie had thought he'd be in a bit of a celebratory mood with the potential killer behind bars.

The knife that Ben had on him had been big enough, wicked enough, to be the murder weapon. Time would tell, but right now Callie was feeling very optimistic about it.

There was no way for them to know the depths of Ben's paranoia. It was very possible that what had driven him to murder were what he perceived were evil threats to him. Maybe when he was interviewed later with his doctor they could find out what might have happened to Ben around Christmas that had made him identify with the holiday song.

However, Mac apparently wasn't feeling it. His silence felt heavy and too thick for her to penetrate with idle conversation. She had never felt such distance from him before and she wished she could see into his brain to see what was going on with him.

When they arrived at Nathan's place his truck was parked in the driveway, letting them know he was waiting for them. He stepped out on his porch as they got out of their car.

"Good morning, Nathan," Mac said.

"Almost afternoon," Nathan replied.

Callie followed Mac up the drive to the porch. "We've got a few more questions for you today. Can we come in?"

Nathan hesitated a moment. "Okay, but today wasn't cleaning day so it's kind of messy inside." He opened the door to allow them inside.

It apparently wasn't cleaning month, Callie thought as she stepped in and looked around. The small living room–kitchen area smelled of garbage. There was no Christmas tree or holiday decorations.

The table was piled high with food wrappers and take-out containers. Clothes covered the only chair in the room, clothes that she couldn't tell if they were clean or dirty. She and Mac sat on the sofa and Nathan pulled in a chair from the kitchen and sat facing them.

"Did you get your toolbox back?" Mac asked.

Nathan nodded. "Deputy Caldwell brought it to me."

"So, what are you working on now?" Mac asked.

"Nothing right now. I'd set aside a couple of days to finish up in Linda's closet but…" His voice trailed off.

"I see you haven't decorated for Christmas," Callie said. "Do you plan on putting up a tree?"

Nathan gave her a winsome smile. "Nah. I figure Christmas is mostly for kids, and since I don't have a wife or kids, there's really no point in putting up a tree."

"How long have you been here in town, Nathan?" Mac asked. "What is it, six…seven years?"

"Actually it's almost eight," Nathan replied. "I lived in Kansas City all my life and when my parents were gone I decided to take off in my rusty truck and see the world."

Mac laughed. "Rock Ridge isn't exactly an exciting place to live. Why here?"

"My truck broke down just out of town and so I ended up staying a couple of days for it to get fixed. Everyone was so nice here. I liked it here…so I stayed." Nathan smiled. "It's a good place to live."

"It isn't so good right now with a killer

on the loose," Mac replied. "And speaking of that…" Mac began the line of questioning into Nathan's alibis for the times of the murders.

Once again Callie focused on Nathan's facial features, trying to discern if he was a liar or not. However, he appeared genuine as he tried to answer Mac's question to the best of his ability. And once again she didn't really believe Nathan had the mental acumen to pull off the murders.

It was after one by the time they made their way back to town. Most of the stores had opened although there weren't many people out and about.

It was the perfect time for her and Mac to hit the stores to see if they could find the five golden rings the killer might be using next. If they could figure that out, then maybe there would be a record of who bought them.

They went into store after store, hunting for the elusive golden rings, but the only place they found them was in the jewelry store for three hundred fifty dollars per ring. A little pricey for five to be left at a murder scene.

"It's possible the killer ordered costume rings off the web," Callie said as they headed back to the office to meet with Dr. Georgino.

"I'm sure there's all kind of party places that sell cheap rings as party favors or whatever."

"With the knife we found on Ben, I should be able to get a search warrant not only for his property, but also all his phone and banking transactions. If he ordered rings online, then we'll find out," Mac replied.

Dr. Georgino was an attractive middle-aged man with black hair, dark eyes and a warm personality that Callie guessed served him well in his profession. He greeted both Mac and Callie warmly. "How's my patient?"

"We're hoping you can tell us," Mac replied. "I had him brought up to the interview room so you can speak to him and perhaps make some assessments. I can't allow you to be with him alone given his unpredictable actions earlier."

"I understand that," the doctor said.

"Then let's go see Ben," Mac replied.

Callie was disappointed that she wasn't invited to sit in for the interview. Instead, she went into the break room. Nobody else was there. She grabbed her purse and pulled out a couple of dollars to buy herself a soda and a bag of roasted peanuts from the vending machine.

As she sank down at the table and began to

munch on the peanuts, her thoughts went over everything that had happened that morning.

She'd been terrified for Mac when Ben had shot at him. She'd been afraid Ben would shoot again and again and Mac would be killed. She really believed they now had their killer behind bars.

The knife that Ben had on him had cinched it for her. With the belief that it was finally over washing through her, a huge weight lifted from her shoulders.

Would Mac now send her back to her desk job? She hoped not. She hoped working the murder cases with him had shown him that she had what it took to be a great deputy. Of course her real dream was to be his wife. But she'd felt his distance from her all afternoon and her hope of being his woman…of him being her man…was slowly diminishing.

She could love him to death, but it didn't matter if he didn't love her back. Certainly their time together over the past two weeks had been so intense with both the highest of highs and lowest of lows. Was it only the stress of the job that had driven Mac into her bed? She didn't want to believe that. In fact, she didn't believe it.

She'd caught him gazing at her on more than one occasion with a softness in his eyes. Beyond the lust he obviously felt toward her, she believed in her very heart and soul that he was falling in love with her. She just hoped he was willing to embrace her love and everything she wanted to bring to his life.

The minutes ticked by and she remained alone in the room and deep into her thoughts. She didn't know how long she remained there before Mac finally walked into the room.

She immediately got to her feet, but he motioned her back down and then sank down in the chair next to hers. "Dr. Georgino just left."

"And?"

"He wants to institute a 5150 process."

Callie raised an eyebrow in surprise. "A seventy-two-hour hold due to mental issues?"

Mac nodded. "He was surprised by the depth of Ben's psychoses…specifically his paranoia. He believes Ben has been off his medication for months and immediately put us on notice as to what Ben needs while he's in our custody."

"So, here's the important question—does the doctor believe Ben is our killer?"

"Before talking to and seeing Ben today, Dr. Georgino believed there was no way Ben could kill anyone. However, after seeing Ben today, he admitted that he couldn't rule it out."

"Hopefully within the next seventy-two hours we'll get forensics back on the knife and we'll be a hundred percent positive that we've got our man."

She leaned forward and placed her hand on his shoulder. "I believe it's over, Mac. I think we have the killer behind bars and the town is safe once again."

He leaned back in the chair and her hand fell away from him. He rubbed the back of his neck and released a deep sigh. "I hope it's over, but in the meantime I have Deputy Roark running background checks on Roger, Ben and Nathan."

"The one thing I'd like to know is what ultimately triggered Ben. I mean, I know it was his mental illness that probably had him kill those women, but why the birds? Why did he identify with that particular Christmas song?"

Mac shook his head. "We may never know the answers to everything." He stood. "And now you're off duty for the day and I'll take you home."

She looked at him in surprise. "But it's only five thirty," she protested.

He smiled. "Welcome to a regular shift."

She got up, walked over to the coat rack and grabbed her coat. She turned to look at him once again. "Are you sure you want me off duty so early? Surely there are still things that need to be done."

"Whatever needs to be done can be done tomorrow. I'm letting several of the others go home on time tonight. We have a viable suspect behind bars. We have seventy-two hours to prove beyond a reasonable doubt that he's our killer and tonight we can all take a breath and then get back hard at work in the morning."

She nodded. "You're the boss." She followed him outside and to his car.

Was it just last night that they had been in each other's arms? Dear God, with everything that had happened today their lovemaking felt as if it had happened months ago.

However, when they got back into the small confines of his car, his scent washed over her, bringing back once again the wonder of being in his arms.

They rode for several moments in silence, but it wasn't the comfortable quiet they occasionally enjoyed. Rather this was the charged silence of things unsaid.

Callie had waited all day to see if Mac would bring up their lovemaking so they could discuss how they each felt after the experience, but now it was obvious he had no intention of bringing it up. So, she would. She couldn't go to sleep without knowing exactly where she stood with him.

He pulled up in front of her house and parked. He turned to gaze at her and in his eyes she saw that softness, that something that made her believe he was in love with her.

"Mac, before we say good-night we have to talk about the elephant in the room," she said.

Immediately his eyes darkened and shuttered against her. "I didn't think there was anything to talk about. I've been clear to you that I'm not looking for a relationship. Last night was wonderful, but it shouldn't have happened."

"But it did happen and it was more than wonderful," she replied. "I… I'm in love with you." The words falling from her lips surprised her. She hadn't meant to let him know just yet how she felt about him. But now the words hung in the air between them.

He shifted in his seat and looked out the front window, obviously uncomfortable. He released a deep sigh and then gazed at her once again, his eyes still dark and impossible to read.

"Callie, the last couple weeks have been intense, and we've spent a lot of time together. Emotions have run high for the both of us, but I think you're now misreading your own feelings."

She stared at him and then released a dry laugh. "Please don't try to undermine my feelings, Mac. I know how I feel about you. I'm in love with you."

He winced, as if he found her words painful. "Don't love me, Callie. You deserve to love a man who can return your love with his whole heart. I don't have a heart that loves. Save your love for somebody who does. And now I think it's best if we just say good-night."

She searched his features for several more moments, seeking some form of softness, some way in beneath the armor he seemed to have drawn around himself. She found none.

"Good night, Mac," she said. "I'll see you first thing in the morning." She got out of the car and opened the back door to retrieve her coat. "She must have done some number on you," she added. She closed the door and headed up the sidewalk and fought back tears of disappointment...of utter heartbreak.

After a night of crying and cursing her heart for falling in love with a man who she believed loved her, but refused to act on it, she was ready to head back into the office.

With a credible suspect behind bars, she wondered whether Mac would put her back on the desk, or keep her as a deputy. If he was now uncomfortable to be in her presence, the best thing for him would be to put her back on the desk, where he only had to have contact with her a couple of times a day.

He'd certainly never promised her a permanent position as a deputy. She'd known all along he'd only appointed her as one because of the situation he'd found himself in with a killer on the loose.

She shoved all these thoughts out of her head and instead steeled herself for seeing Mac again after the conversation they'd had the night before. Opening her door, she stepped outside into the bright sunshine.

She immediately saw Nathan's truck parked at the curb and Nathan on the ground, hunched over and holding his ankle. "Nathan, what happened?" she asked as she took several steps toward him.

"I was on my way to Jason Donovan's house to do some work and I thought I had a flat tire. I parked to get out and look and slipped and twisted my ankle."

He looked like a pathetic little boy sitting

in the snow with a stocking cap askew on his head and his eyes filled with hurt. "Can I call somebody to help you?" Callie asked.

"I don't have anyone to call," he replied. "I just need to get in my truck and go home." He tried to stand, but fell back in the snow. "Could you just help me to the driver's door?"

Callie hesitated a moment and looked around. There was nobody out on the snowy streets at this time of the morning. She felt no real threat from Nathan. She'd always believed he wasn't bright enough to pull off the murders.

She touched the butt of her gun to assure herself and then approached where Nathan sat. When she reached him he threw his arm around her shoulder and moaned slightly.

With her help he managed to get to his feet and together with him leaning on her they got to the driver's door. He turned back to her. "Thanks for your help, Deputy Stevens," he said.

He made a quick movement and something sharp stuck Callie in her thigh. "Ouch… What…?" She looked down to see a hypodermic needle. She looked up at Nathan in surprise.

His eyes were no longer innocuous, but

rather filled with a sly cunning. She fumbled at her side, wanting to pull her weapon, but it felt as if she was moving through sludge.

Her vision blurred as Nathan grabbed her gun from her holster. Her heartbeat slowed despite the fear that filled her.

Her muscles refused to work with her brain and her knees suddenly weakened. She felt herself falling, but Nathan caught her. He picked her up in his arms and carried her to the back of his pickup.

Danger. Oh God, she was in danger. Nathan wasn't on Mac's radar anymore. Nathan began to hum "The Twelve Days of Christmas" song, chilling her to her bones.

She fought to stay conscious, but she was completely boneless and a frightening darkness crept in. Nathan placed her in the bed of the truck and then covered her with a blue tarp.

Help me! The words screamed in her head. As the darkness overtook her, her last conscious, horrifying thought was that she was going to be the five golden rings… She was going to die.

Chapter Twelve

The brief conversation with Callie last night had played and replayed in Mac's head all night long. He'd felt her love for him pouring from her. He'd wanted to pull her into his arms and kiss her all night long. He'd wanted to tell her that he was deeply in love with her, but he hadn't. He couldn't.

The blow Amanda had delivered to his heart that Christmas Eve when she'd walked out on him had forever scarred him. He'd been truthful when he'd told Callie he had no heart to give her.

She deserved to have a man who could love her with all his heart and soul. She deserved so much more than what Mac could give her.

It was just after six when he sat at the kitchen table and drank a cup of coffee before going into work. His mind raced with thoughts, both about the murders and about Callie.

Did they have the right man in jail right now? Had Ben committed the murders while in a fugue state due to him going off his medication and becoming trapped in a depth of paranoia about evil spirits?

How would things go with Callie when she came in this morning? Would she be embarrassed by her profession of her love for him the night before? Would she be hurt and wear that hurt in her beautiful eyes? God, he wasn't sure he could stand that. The last thing he'd ever wanted to do was hurt her.

He recognized that he was guilty of giving her mixed messages. He'd told her he wasn't interested in a relationship and yet he'd touched her in loving ways, and he'd kissed her and made love with her.

He stared out the window where the rising sun reflected red and orange on the snow. He hoped he heard from forensics today that the knife taken off Ben was the murder weapon. That would seal the deal on Ben's guilt and the young women in the town would once again be safe.

With this thought in mind he finished up his coffee and then pulled on his coat as thoughts of Callie returned to his mind. If he knew her as much as he thought he did, then she would come in first thing this morning with her head held high.

He couldn't help but smile with this thought. She had more strength, more spunk than any other woman he had ever known and that was part of what he loved about her.

He got to the office and went directly to his desk. He needed to check his email to see if any reports had come in. Unfortunately, there was nothing. He'd have to be patient and in the meantime he'd make sure his deputies were still questioning people about the murders.

Even though he'd pretty much written off Roger and Nathan as suspects, that didn't mean that more questioning might not turn up another suspect. They also needed to begin to build a case against Ben if he was their man.

They needed to find out what his actions were on the date of every murder. Any alibi he had for the days and nights had to be checked and rechecked.

He was vaguely surprised when eight o'clock rolled around and Callie still wasn't in. He held his morning meeting with all his other deputies and once they all had their assignments they left.

Mac put his coat back on and got into his car. He wanted people to see him out and about. He needed them to know that he was still working on their behalf. He drove up and down the streets, making notes of areas that hadn't seen a snowplow yet.

It was after ten when he returned to the office, shocked that Callie still hadn't come in. It wasn't like her. Even with the conversation they'd had the night before, it wasn't like her to avoid him. It definitely wasn't like her to blow off work.

He finally called her, but the call went to her voice mail and he hung up. A half an hour later he called her again with the same results, but this time he left her a message. "Callie, where are you? I figured you would already be here. Call me back and let me know what's going on." He hung up, dissatisfied with the message and with the fact that she wasn't answering her phone.

Had the fact that he'd told her he had no heart to give her somehow broken her? God, he hoped not. He couldn't imagine seeing her without the sparkle in her eyes, without that optimistic smile on her face. Surely she was stronger than that. Dammit, he knew she was stronger than that. So, where was she?

It was just after eleven when the faint niggle of worry he had about her became too big to ignore. He got back in his car and headed over to her house. He parked in her driveway and headed for her front door.

Nothing appeared amiss. He knocked on the door loud enough for the neighbors to hear. No reply. He knocked again. "Callie, come to the door," he yelled. Still no response from her.

He waited several minutes and then headed back to his car. Maybe she was inside the house and just not answering any calls from him. With this thought in mind he headed toward Janie's Stuff and Things. He knew from idle conversation with Callie that she and Janie were close friends.

He wasn't one to put his personal business on blast, but the truth was he was worried about Callie and just needed to know she was okay. Hopefully Callie would answer a call from her friend.

The store was open even though there were few people out and about on the snowy sidewalks. The moment he walked into the store he was surrounded by Christmas, which immediately evoked thoughts of Callie and her home.

"Sheriff." Janie greeted him with a warm

smile. "Fancy seeing you in here. Are you looking for a special gift for somebody?"

"Actually, I'm hoping you would do me a favor." He hesitated a moment, wondering if he had completely lost his mind. Still, all he wanted was to know that Callie was okay. "Uh… I know you and Callie are good friends. Have you talked to her at all today?"

"No. Why, is something wrong?" Janie immediately appeared worried.

"She hasn't come in to work today and she didn't call in to say she wasn't coming. I went by her house and knocked, but she didn't answer. I've also called her several times but she isn't answering my calls." The words fell out of his mouth faster than he could edit himself.

"We…we had a conversation last night that might have upset her, so she might not want to talk to me right now so I was wondering if maybe you could call her and make sure she's okay. Surely she would answer your call."

Janie grabbed a black purse from behind the counter and pulled out her cell phone. "No matter what happened between the two of you, it's not like her to blow off work. Callie has always been the utmost professional when it comes to her job."

Janie opened her phone case and punched

a button that would ring Callie. Mac waited, hoping...praying...that Callie would answer and he'd know she was okay.

However, the phone rang several times and then went to voice mail. Janie frowned. "Let me try her again." Janie punched the button again and got the same result. "I'm sorry, Mac. Maybe she's busy with something or in the shower. I'll keep trying her."

"Thanks, and could you let me know when you hear from her?"

"For sure. I'll call and let you know," Janie replied.

As Mac left the shop, the alarm bells that had been ringing about Callie grew louder. What if they had the wrong man in jail? What if Ben wasn't the killer?

A vision of Callie filled his head... Callie with her blond curls... Callie who was the perfect fit for the killer's victimology.

As he got into his car he hoped and prayed that he was wrong, that Ben was their killer and Callie was someplace safe. However, as he drove back to the office the alarm in his head screeched.

One way or another he had to find Callie. If what he feared was true, then he only had a matter of hours before she would be stabbed to death and left someplace on the street with a Santa hat on her head and five golden rings on her fingers.

CALLIE CAME TO in bits and increments. The smell hit her first…the dank scent of earth… the noxious smells of blood and death. Her mind worked to make sense of it. Where was she?

She cracked open her eyes and fought through the fog in her brain. She was in a root cellar of sorts. She opened her eyes wider despite a headache that rolled across her forehead.

There was a workbench against one wall, shelving on the other wall and she was on a bunk bed. The workbench held a lamp that illuminated the area. She started to get up and realized her arms and feet were tied to the bed.

Sheer panic screamed through her. What had happened? How had she gotten here? Oh God…what was going on? And then she remembered. Nathan and his pretense of a hurt ankle.

Oh God, she'd been so stupid. She'd fallen for a ruse she should have never fallen for. She hadn't believed he had the acumen to be the killer, and yet here she was.

She strained against the ropes that tied her

wrists to the bed frame. There was no give. She attempted to move her legs, but the rope around her ankles held tight.

She spied a pile of coats and purses in the corner of the room. They were items that belonged to the murdered women and her white winter coat was on top. The sheet beneath her felt stiff and as she moved her body to one side and peered down at it, she saw the reason for the stiffness. Blood...old, dried blood. They'd wondered where the killing place was and now she knew. Panic once again soared through her and she kicked and pulled against the binds that held her until she was breathless.

Where was Nathan now? She looked toward the slanted wooden door. The next time she saw him would he come down with a knife in his hand, ready to stab her to death?

A deep sob welled up and exploded out of her. She was in trouble. When she hadn't shown up for work that morning had Mac just figured she was avoiding him? After their conversation the night before had he believed she was mad at him and that's why she hadn't come in to work?

Did he even know she was missing? Another sob escaped her. Was anybody even looking for her? She didn't want to die. She didn't want to be another victim.

Tears chased each other down her cheeks as she frantically tugged at the ropes. Somehow…some way…she had to escape. She had to get off of the bed and out the door.

She couldn't depend on anyone to find her, especially if they didn't even know that she was missing. Somehow she needed to save herself, but at the moment she wasn't sure how to do that.

She had no idea what time it was, but she knew it was only a matter of hours before Nathan would come at her with a knife. If nothing changed, then she knew she was on a countdown to her own death.

With that thought in mind, she began to scream for help…hoping and praying that somebody would hear her cries.

BY THE TIME he got back to the office, Mac was frantic. His fear for Callie was a living, breathing thing inside him. He put all his deputies on alert to be on the watch for her and then he hit the road again.

The first place he drove was to Roger's insurance company. Roger's car was parked out front and as Mac slowly drove by he could see Roger inside the office.

On his drive to Nathan's place, he tried to call Callie again and got the message that her voice mail was full. That only sent his fear for her higher. Where could she be? He couldn't believe she was just out walking around the snow-filled streets of the town or hiding out in her house.

He believed it was quite possible that the serial killer who had terrorized the town now had Callie in his clutches. His stomach muscles clenched tightly at the very thought.

When he got to Nathan's place the man's truck wasn't there. Mac returned to town and drove up and down the streets until he found Nathan's vehicle parked at the curb of Jason and Margaret Donovan's house. Mac got out of his truck and hurried to the front door. Jason answered. "Is Nathan here?" Mac asked before Jason could even greet him properly.

"Yes, he's doing a little work in our kitchen. Is there a problem?" Jason asked.

"What time did he get here today?" Mac asked.

Jason frowned. "I'm not sure, I think it was around nine or so. Is there a problem?" he asked again.

"No, but do you mind if I speak with him?" Mac asked.

"Of course not... Come on in." Jason opened the door wider to allow Mac entry. He followed Jason through an attractive living room and into a large, airy kitchen. Margaret was seated at the table with a cup of coffee in front of her and Nathan appeared to be changing the hardware on the cabinets.

"Margaret," he greeted her.

"Good afternoon, Sheriff," she said in obvious surprise.

"Hey, Nathan, how's it going for you?" Mac said.

Nathan offered him his usual smile. "Can't complain," he replied.

"I was wondering if you saw Deputy Stevens this morning?" Mac watched the man carefully.

"Deputy Stevens?" Nathan looked at him with what appeared to be confusion. "Why would I see her this morning? Was I supposed to see her?"

"No, I was just wondering if you had. She seems to be missing," Mac replied.

"Missing?" Margaret looked at him worriedly. "Is it possible...? Do you think...?"

"I don't know what to think, but we're actively searching for her now. I just figured Nathan was probably up and around earlier this morning so he might have seen her."

"Sorry, but I didn't see her anywhere around," Nathan replied.

"Then I'll just be on my way. Thanks, folks." Mac hurried back to the front door and to his car. As he drove away, a lump of despair filled the back of his throat.

Nathan would have been his biggest suspect, but he was in a kitchen changing hardware on cabinets instead of holding Callie somewhere to wait for killing time.

She walked to work every morning. She would have been vulnerable to being kidnapped off the street. Why in the hell hadn't he been picking her up every morning to make sure she wasn't exposed to a killer?

And if not Roger or Nathan, then who? The investigation had yielded no other suspects. He didn't know where to begin to find her. But dammit, if he had to break down every door in the entire town, he would do it to get to her.

According to the previous four murders, the women had been killed between the hours of seven and nine in the evening. It was now almost two. That gave him and his team five hours to find her before she'd be found dead and posed on the street.

Chapter Thirteen

Callie didn't know how long she screamed before she ultimately stopped. She finally realized if she was being held someplace around Nathan's house, then there was nobody around to hear her cries for help.

Minutes ticked by…agonizing minutes that ticked off her very life. She had no idea what time it was, but it felt as if hours had gone by.

She continued to tug and pull at the ropes until she felt the warmth of her own blood, to no avail. There was nothing she could do but wait for Nathan to return. As she awaited her own death, her head filled with myriad thoughts.

At least in death she would be reunited with the family she had lost. She would once again feel her father's strong arms around her and her mother's loving kiss on her cheek. She'd throw her arms around her little sister and hold her until they were both giggling.

However, as much as she loved her family and as much as she wanted to be reunited with them some day, she wasn't ready for it right now. She wanted to live to get married. She wanted to know the joy of childbirth and being a mother.

She'd been hoping for more time to make Mac realize they belonged together and that whatever had happened in his past had nothing to do with the never-ending love she had for him. She truly believed it was just a matter of time before he'd realize he could trust her and embrace not only the love she had for him, but also the love she knew he had for her.

But time had run out for her…for them. Tears once again blurred her eyes, tears of hopelessness, of loss. She would never again hear the wonderful sound of Mac's deep laughter, or fall into the soft gray shades of his eyes.

She wouldn't know anymore the wonder of being held in Mac's arms, the complete joy of him kissing her. She would never have the pleasure of making love with him again. And she wept uncontrollably at these thoughts.

She didn't want to die this way. It was going to be an excruciating way to die. She was going to be stabbed over and over and over again. She could only pray that the first stab killed her, that she wasn't alive or conscious for additional stabs wounds.

How frightened the others must have been to be tied down and know they were going to be stabbed to death. They hadn't even known it was because they were blondes and fit the victimology of a disturbed man.

Finally, she had no more tears to shed. Her wrists and ankles burned and hurt and she was exhausted by her efforts to get free.

She must have fallen asleep for the sound of snow crunching beneath footsteps awakened her. Every muscle in her body froze as the cellar door creaked open, footsteps sounded on a couple of the stairs and then the door fell shut.

Nathan walked down the stairs and turned to look at her. It was Nathan and yet it wasn't Nathan. Gone was the slight emptiness in his eyes and the cheerful smile that usually played on his face.

Instead, his eyes were filled with a shrewdness and his mouth was a slash of tight-lipped anger that only made her fear flame hotter.

He stared at her for several long, heart-pounding moments. "Ashley, why won't you ever die?" he finally said. "I've tried to get rid of you over and over again, but you keep reappearing."

"Nathan, I'm not Ashley. I'm Deputy Stevens… Callie… Remember me?" She forced a smile. "I'm Callie and I don't know Ashley."

"Shut up," he snapped. "I don't want to hear anything coming out of your lying mouth. I want you to shut up and listen and understand exactly what you did to me."

He began to pace in front of the bed. His short, quick steps, along with one of his hands racing through his hair over and over again, spoke of his deep agitation.

He stopped again in front of her and held out his hand. She was surprised to see a wedding band on his finger. It was a gold band with tiny diamondlike chips all around it. Callie knew he was missing a chip… It had been found at a murder scene. But nobody else knew that.

"You gave me this ring and promised before God and all our friends that you would love me forever. You remember that, Ashley? You remember all the promises you made?" He spoke deceptively soft.

"Please, Nathan. I'm not Ashley."

His unexpected slap to her face instantly made her cry out in pain as tears filled her eyes. "I told you to shut up. You can't fool me, Ashley. It was bad enough that you broke our wedding vows and divorced me. But then you killed my son." He practically screamed the words at her.

Despite her pain…in spite of her fear… Callie looked at Nathan in surprise. She needed to know what exactly had happened to Nathan that had turned him into a cold-blooded killer.

"Nathan, tell me, how did your son die?" she asked and then winced as she waited for another slap to her face.

Instead of slapping her for speaking, he began to pace once again. "You know how he died. You were the one responsible."

"Let's talk about it, Nathan," she said softly. Not only did she want to know what had happened, but she also wanted to keep him talking for as long as possible. Even though she knew she was entertaining false hope, she wanted to believe that somebody… anybody…might rescue her in time.

"You know what you did, Ashley. After you left me, we shared custody of little David and you had him for Christmas Eve. You put him in a bathtub and then you answered a phone call. While you chatted on the phone, our little boy slipped under the water and drowned. His safety wasn't as important as your damned phone call." Anguish filled his voice. "He died while you were on a damned phone call."

"Oh, Nathan, I'm so sorry." A deep sadness swept through her at his story…for his pain. "Nathan, I'm so sorry for your loss." So, he'd lost his son on Christmas Eve. That explained Christmas being his trigger. What about the song? "What's important about 'The Twelve Days of Christmas' song?"

He stopped pacing and glared at her. "Don't you remember anything? That damned song was playing in the background when you called to tell me my son was dead." His hands clenched and unclenched at his sides.

So, now she understood all the dynamics of his crimes. She comprehended the overkill present with each victim. What she somehow needed for him to understand was that she wasn't his ex-wife… She wasn't his Ashley, who he apparently thought needed to be punished by death.

"Nathan, I'm so sorry about what happened to you. I'm sorry your wife left you and I'm sorry your son died in what sounds like a tragic accident," she said, trying to keep her panic out of her voice. "Nathan, please look at me. I'm not your wife. I'm not Ashley."

"You lie," he screamed. He twirled around from her and grabbed a knife from the top of the workbench. Her breath caught in the back of her throat. "You keep lying to me over and over again. I keep killing you but you come right back again. You're a damned demon woman and you have to be killed once and for all."

He stabbed the knifepoint into the bench, making Callie jump and release a heart-stopping gasp. "You killed my little boy and for that alone you have to die. I hear him crying in my dreams, I have nightmares about him being under the water and not being able to breathe. I watch him die night after night while that damned Christmas song plays over and over again."

"Nathan, killing me isn't going to make it stop. You need help, Nathan. You need to talk to a doctor. He would help you realize that killing Ashley over and over again isn't working for you. It isn't helping you with your grief." She tried to keep her voice calm, despite her need to scream.

He stared at her for a long moment, causing her breath to catch below her ribs and making it impossible for her to breathe. He grabbed the knife once again.

"You don't understand. I have no other

choice. I have to stop the nightmares. I have to make it right. My little boy needs justice and killing you is the only way he'll get it." He turned his wrist over and looked at his watch.

He gazed back at her, his eyes dark and dead. "It was eight o'clock when I got the call that our son was dead. You have an hour and a half to ask for atonement and to pray for your sins. Then the knife of justice will come for you."

He placed the knife back on the workbench and then reached into his pocket and pulled out a handful of little bright golden rings, making her gasp painfully once again.

He stared down at the rings, put them back in his pocket and then headed toward the stairs. "Nathan…wait. Just let me go, Nathan. I'm not Ashley. Please just let me go," she said, begging and pleading.

He whirled back around, anger once again flashing in his eyes. "I've told you over and over again to shut up. Now I'm going to make sure you shut up."

He grabbed a roll of duct tape from the workbench, ripped off a couple of pieces and then pressed them tightly against her mouth. As he walked up the stairs she screamed against the tape. He reached the top, opened the door and stepped out and then slammed the door shut behind him.

IT WAS JUST after six and Mac was frantic. Nobody had seen Callie all day long and Mac was absolutely convinced she'd been kidnapped and was now being held by the killer. He knew time was running out for her. What he didn't know was the identity of the killer.

All afternoon his deputies had been out knocking on doors in search of their fellow deputy. They had checked out empty sheds and barns seeking the place where women had been held and then murdered. They found nothing.

It was as if Callie had disappeared into thin air. But, dammit, she had to be somewhere. He now sat in the break room going over everything and waiting for a few of his deputies to check in for new orders.

He didn't know what new orders to give them. Find Callie. That's all he wanted— that's all he needed. He couldn't imagine never seeing her smiling face again. He couldn't stand the thought of never hearing her laughter again. His fear was so great for her it filled his chest almost to the point that he couldn't speak.

He loved her and the thought of her being murdered…stabbed to death…caused a wealth of grief to bring tears to his eyes. He felt so helpless.

What little evidence they had, had been gone over a million times. The hunt for additional suspects had yielded nothing. The tears raced faster from his eyes and he angrily swiped at them. Now wasn't the time for him to get emotional or break down. He needed action.

Dammit, where could she be? Who was holding her with the intent of killing her? The minutes ticked by…ticking down to Callie's death. He consciously shoved his grief aside and once again focused on the paperwork before him.

Roger and Nathan had been two of his leading suspects. But both of them had worked all day. When would they have had time to kidnap Callie and hold her someplace all day long?

He supposed one of them could have kidnapped her the moment she'd stepped out her door that morning. That person could have taken her somewhere and then left her to go to work to establish an alibi.

He wasn't sure why his thoughts kept returning to Nathan. He wasn't even sure the man was capable of committing these crimes, and yet Mac kept going back to him.

Johnny came in, his face as troubled as Mac's thoughts. "Nothing," he said and threw himself into the chair next to Mac's. "I checked half a dozen sheds and any building that might be the hidey-hole place of the killer. Where could she be, Mac?"

"God, I wish I knew," Mac replied. "I have this ticking clock in my chest and once it ticks down to detonation it's going to rip a huge hole through my heart."

Johnny looked at him for a long moment. "You know she's crazy about you."

"I'm pretty crazy about her, too." The words fell from Mac before he could edit himself. He released a deep sigh. "But it doesn't matter how I feel about her if we don't find her in time." His chest tightened, making it difficult for him to draw a breath.

He glanced toward the window where dusk had fallen with night soon to follow. The clock inside his head ticked louder. "Maybe we should run by Roger's and Nathan's places and check in with them again," Mac finally said.

"Whatever you want, boss. I'd love to go put the squeeze on sleazy Roger and I know all the deputies are behind you in whatever you need from us," Johnny replied.

"Sheriff," Deputy Andy Roark said urgently as he entered the breakroom, "I think I got him." He handed Mac a printed piece of paper. "This article appeared in the *Kansas City Star* almost eight years ago."

Mac looked at the copy with the headline: "Christmas Eve Tragedy." The article talked about the drowning death of a four-month-old baby. The mother, twenty-five-year-old Ashley Morton, had put the baby in the tub for a bath and unfortunately, she'd turned her back to take a phone call and when she turned back to attend to the baby, he had drowned. Ashley was newly divorced from the baby's father, Nathan Brighton. There was a photo of Ashley. She was an attractive blonde.

All of Mac's muscles froze. It was Nathan. He looked at Johnny. "Get all the men together and meet me in the Halloway driveway." The Halloways' home was the closest to Nathan's. "Nathan should be home by now. We'll meet and formulate a plan to go in without risking Callie's life."

They all moved at the same time, heading for the exit and to their own cars. Nathan. It had to be Nathan. The tragic event in his past at Christmastime had triggered him into a killing spree. And Callie was his next victim.

He drove faster than he'd ever driven before, thankful there was little traffic on the roads. He pulled up in the Halloway drive and then waited for his men to arrive, praying that they weren't already too late. God... they had to get to her in time.

ONCE AGAIN, SHE HEARD his footsteps approaching. Her heart beat so rapidly she felt nauseous. She began to weep, knowing it was time. He was coming to stab her to death. She couldn't help but pray that the first wound killed her quickly. She didn't want to live through twenty-five or twenty-six stabbings.

The door opened and as Nathan closed it behind him, she thrashed on the bed trying with all her power to break free. She screamed once again, the screams trapped in the duct tape that held her mouth closed.

Nathan walked into her view. His eyes were dark and simmering with what appeared to be suppressed rage. "It's time, Ashley...time for my son to get his justice. You should have never put our little boy in the bathtub and then turned your back on him to talk on your phone."

He stepped close to her, his face mere inches from her own. "Who was on the phone, bitch?" he screamed. "Who was more important than our baby boy? Who called you that was so damned important that you had to talk to them instead of taking care of our son? Was it your boyfriend? Huh? Was that who it was, you bitch?"

He backed away until he hit the worktable behind him. "Hopefully you won't come back again. Once I kill you, I hope you stay dead. I need you to stay dead once and for all."

His words only torched her terror higher. Within minutes she would feel the agony of a knife piercing through her. She now realized intimately what the other victims had experienced in the minutes before their deaths. Her heart cried out not only with her own horror, but with theirs, as well.

"You made me have to do this," Nathan continued to rage. "It's all your fault that I have to kill you. You should have never turned your back on my little boy. He was the best thing that had ever happened to me and once he was gone my whole life fell apart."

He whirled around to the workbench. He grabbed up the knife once again and then turned to face her. "I loved you once, Ashley. I loved you with all my heart. But you left me. I could hate you for that alone, but I really hate you for not taking care of my child. I hate you... Do you hear me? I hate you."

He raised the knife and Callie tensed. As if in slow motion she watched the knife come down and then stab into the side of her stomach. Excruciating pain seared through her. She screamed and then gasped against the tape over her mouth.

She was dying. Her mind worked to comprehend the fact that at this very moment she was being murdered by the very serial killer she had sought to find.

The knife stabbed into her again. An agonizing pain once again fired through her and she felt the warmth of the blood leaving her body. Tears wept from the corner of her eyes and she prayed for unconsciousness... for a quick death.

He raised the knife and was about to stab her again when a faint knocking sound stopped his knife movement. He threw the knife on the workbench and hurried up and out of the cellar.

Callie continued to weep with pain and the horrifying knowledge that he'd be back to finish the job.

Chapter Fourteen

Mac knocked on Nathan's door. He'd decided to come in soft with just Johnny by his side, rather than storming the house with all his men. However, those men were now scattered in the woods around Nathan's place just waiting for Mac's call for them.

The darkness of night had fallen, making Mac aware that every minute counted. He knocked again, harder this time, and finally Nathan came to the door.

"Sheriff," Nathan greeted him with his usual wide-eyed innocence. "What are you doing here?"

"I'm here for Callie," Mac replied. All his senses were working overtime. He shot a glance around. The bedroom door was open, but he didn't sense anyone in there. He sniffed the air, but didn't smell a trace of her perfume. He heard nothing that would indicate a woman was in the house and struggling to get free.

"Callie? Why would you think she's here?" Nathan asked, an eyebrow quirked up in confusion. "Did she tell you she was coming here?"

Mac knew with certainty Nathan was their man. He had Callie hidden away someplace. Were they too late? Is that why Mac didn't feel her spirit, her essence anywhere?

"Nathan, cut the crap. We know everything. We know about your son and we know you killed those women. Now, where is Callie?"

The innocence in Nathan's eyes disappeared and instead a dark madness filled them. Before Mac could guess the man's next move, he turned and raced toward his bedroom. He crashed through the window and disappeared from sight.

"Dammit! Call the men," Mac yelled to Johnny as he raced for the bedroom and then dived through the broken window. Once he got to his feet, he turned on his flashlight and shone the light around him to get his bearings.

He immediately spied a root cellar door in the back of the house. Callie. He knew she was down there. He also saw a padlock on the door. His emotional side told him to get to her, but his intellectual side told him to go after the killer, get him under arrest and get the key to Nathan's lair.

There was nothing he could do for Callie right now, but if Nathan somehow managed to escape, then a killer would be on the loose. Mac raced after Nathan. Thankfully between his flashlight and the moonlight spilling down from overhead he could see the man racing for the trees in the distance.

Mac's heart beat frantically as he ran faster than he'd ever run in his life. The faster they got Nathan in custody, the faster he could get to Callie.

Were they too late? Had Nathan already killed Callie? Oh God, he couldn't think that way. Nathan reached the tree line and Deputy Cameron Royal jumped out from behind a tree trunk and slammed Nathan to the ground.

Mac raced to where the two men grappled on the ground. He grabbed one of Nathan's arms and jerked the man to his feet. Rage filled Mac as he thought about what Nathan had done to the victims…to Mac's town. He got Nathan into handcuffs.

He wanted to smash his fist into Nathan's face. He wanted to shoot the man a dozen times, but what he wanted more than anything was the key to the root cellar.

"Where's the key?" Mac was vaguely aware of his men closing in around them. "Where's the damned key to the root cellar?" Nathan merely grinned…a wicked, sick smile.

Mac reached into Nathan's left pocket and found nothing. He checked his right pocket and found a key ring with dozens of keys on it.

"Get him out of here," he said to Cameron. "Take him to jail and out of my sight."

Mac ran, along with half of his men, for the cellar. Mac's heart pounded so hard he felt half-nauseous. She had to be all right. She just had to be. When he reached the root cellar, his fingers fumbled through the keys, seeking the one that would unlock the door.

He tried three small keys before he found the right one. The padlock released and Mac threw it to the side. He yanked open the door and instantly smelled the scent of blood and death and knew that this was Nathan's killing place.

He ran down the stairs and stopped at the bottom. Callie was tied to the frame of the twin bed. Her eyes were closed, her face pale as death, and her khaki blouse had blood on it.

Oh God, he was too late. He nearly fell to his knees as a deep grief pierced through him. She was gone. She'd been stabbed to death.

And then he heard it…a soft moan. "Call for an ambulance," he yelled up the stairs.

"Callie." He ran to her side. "Callie, honey. We're here and you're safe now. Can you open your eyes for me?" How badly had she been hurt? Was she dying right now in front of him? "Callie…please open your eyes and look at me." He pulled the tape off her mouth.

She moaned once again and then he was looking into her beautiful blue eyes. She stared at him for a long moment. "Am I dead?" Her voice was a slow whisper.

"No, honey. You aren't dead and we're going to get you out of here," Mac replied.

"I hurt, Mac. He stabbed me and I'm dying but I… I need to tell you that I'll love you through eternity." Her eyes drifted closed again.

"Callie… Callie stay with me," Mac cried. He looked at Johnny, who had come down the stairs behind him. "See if you can find something to cut her loose," Mac said.

Johnny moved to the workbench. "There's a big knife here with blood on it."

"Find something else to use. That's our murder weapon," Mac replied tersely. Johnny found a second knife and handed it to Mac.

Callie's wrists were bloody from her obvious struggles against the ropes. The sight made Mac's heart squeeze tight. As he worked on the ropes that bound her, he continued to call her name, but she appeared to be unconscious.

He was scared to death. Were they really too late after all? Once he got the ropes off her he feared that any attempt to move her might do more damage. He had no idea how many times she'd been stabbed.

Thankfully, at that moment two paramedics came down the stairs with a stretcher in their hands. Mac and Johnny went upstairs so the two men could work to bring Callie up and to the waiting ambulance.

Mac's heart banged hard against his ribs. All the love he had for her flooded through him. All he wanted right now was for her to be okay.

The minute she was loaded into the ambulance, Mac got into his car and followed the blue-and-red swirling lights on top of the emergency vehicle as the siren released its loud song.

Tears burned at his eyes...tears of stress

and the relief that finally the killer was behind bars. Mostly his tears were for Callie. Was she going to survive this horrendous day and night? Or in the end would she be just another victim of a serial killer?

"No," the word exploded from his lips. She had to be okay. She just had to be.

When they reached the hospital, the ambulance disappeared into its bay and Mac pulled into the closest parking space in front of the emergency room doors.

He sat in his car for a moment, wrestling to get his emotions under control. The last thing he wanted was for any of his men…anyone at all…to see him weak. But his love for Callie made him weak. He finally got himself under some semblance of control and then left his car and hurried into the emergency room waiting area.

Lana Albright was behind the receptionist desk. She was in her mid-fifties and had worked as the nighttime receptionist for as long as Mac could remember. "Lana, they just brought in Deputy Callie Stevens. Can you tell the doctor on call that I'm waiting here for an update on her condition?"

"It's Dr. Washburn on duty tonight and I'll go back and let them know you're out here." She immediately got up from the desk and disappeared behind a door that read No Entry.

Mac was glad it was Dr. Eric Washburn on duty. He was an older man and Mac trusted his expertise completely. Mac sank down in one of the green plastic chairs, nerves racing through him.

Was she going to be all right? She hadn't regained consciousness as they'd loaded her into the ambulance and that had scared the hell out of him.

He had no idea just how many times Nathan had stabbed her. Thank God he'd knocked on Nathan's door when he had. A minute or two later might have really been too late for Callie. He wasn't sure now that it hadn't been too late.

He buried his face in his hands, another wave of grief stabbing through him. He couldn't imagine never seeing her bright smile again, never hearing her optimism ringing in her voice. He just couldn't imagine not having her in his life ever again.

The sound of the emergency room door whooshing open caused him to sit up. Johnny looked at him worriedly. Johnny and Adam Cook entered. "Any word on her condition?" Adam asked worriedly.

Johnny sank down on one side of Mac and

Adam sat on the other side of him. "Nothing yet," Mac replied. "Nathan locked up tight?"

"He is, although I really wanted to beat the hell out of him for what he'd done," Adam said.

"That makes two of us," Mac said.

"Uh…make that three," Johnny replied with unbridled anger in his tone.

"All I care about now is Callie's well-being," Mac said.

"That's what everyone cares about," Johnny said. "We've got to get back on the roads, but we wanted you to know that we're all worried about Callie." The two men stood.

"If you call me and let me know how she's doing, then I'll let all the deputies know because they're all concerned about her."

Minutes later Mac was once again alone in the waiting room. He wasn't surprised the other deputies were worried about Callie. It just reminded him that Callie had touched everyone with her warmth and bright spirit.

The minutes ticked by…agonizing minutes that turned into one hour and then two. What was happening? What was taking so long? How many stab wounds had she received?

Finally, Dr. Washburn walked out. Mac leaped to his feet, his heart hammering in his chest. "Dr. Washburn, how is she?"

"She had one knife wound that thankfully missed all vital organs. However, the second wound stabbed into her spleen, forcing me to perform an emergency splenectomy. Other than that, she was also suffering from shock and loss of blood."

"But she's going to be okay?" Mac asked.

For the first time Dr. Washburn smiled. "Barring any complications, she should be just fine. It will take her about six weeks to fully recover from the surgery and be ready again for active duty, but she's resting peacefully."

"Can I see her?" Mac asked.

"She'll be groggy from the anesthesia and I certainly don't want her to be stressed."

"I just want to peek in on her." Mac desperately wanted to see her and assure himself she was really okay.

"She's in room 110."

Before the doctor could say anything else, Mac was hurrying down the hallway to Callie's room. When he reached it, he stopped in the doorway.

The room was in semidarkness. She looked tiny in the big bed with white sheets pulled up around her and an IV drip connected to one arm. Her blond curls formed a halo around her head and she appeared as if she were sleeping peacefully.

She'd been through hell and back in this single day. *I'll love you through eternity.* Her words played and replayed in his mind. She'd believed she was dying and had used her last breath to tell him that.

And now he was going to have to figure out what he was going to do about that, but in the meantime, he had a murder scene to process and a case to build to make sure that Nathan went away for the rest of his life.

CALLIE JERKED AWAKE, flailing her arms and legs in an effort to get free from the ropes before Nathan could come and finish her off. It took her only a moment to realize she was fighting against an IV line in her arm and tangled sheets around her feet.

She sagged back against the mattress as she realized she was safe. A glance out the window let her know it must be around noon. Noon of what day? Not only was she disoriented as to day and time, but also to find herself in the hospital.

She closed her eyes again and tried to remember what had happened. Snippets of memories began to fire off in her mind. Nathan, screaming in her face and then stabbing her. She still felt the pain of his stab wounds.

There had been a knock…and then Mac crashing down the stairs…and then…and then nothing. It was obvious from where she was now that she'd been saved.

So, what damage had she sustained? Her wrists and ankles burned, but she couldn't see how badly they'd been hurt because her wrists were wrapped up in bandages. Her stomach also hurt. How badly had Nathan damaged her before she'd been rescued?

She opened her eyes once again and raised the head of her bed a bit. At that moment Dana Johnson walked in. Callie had met nurse Dana when some of the hospital staff had come to the sheriff's office to brush up CPR skills with everyone.

"Ah, good. You're awake," Dana greeted with a bright smile. "How are you feeling?"

"Okay, I guess, although I'm having some pain."

Dana moved to her side with a machine that held everything necessary to take vitals. "On a scale of one to ten, how would you rate your pain level right now?"

"Maybe about a seven," Callie confessed.

"Let me get these vitals and I'll speak to the doctor about some pain meds. He'll be in later to speak to you, but in the meantime, we should be able to make you more comfortable."

Dana left and then returned about ten minutes later with pain meds that she inserted into Callie's IV. Almost immediately Callie's pain eased up and her eyes drifted closed.

She must have fallen asleep because the next thing she knew a woman came in serving her lunch. She introduced herself as Wendy. "There's a grilled chicken sandwich and a nice cup of soup for you," she said. "But if you need or want anything else, you just let me know. You're a real hero and it's my honor to serve you."

"Wendy, I'm no hero. The real hero in all this is Mac and his team of hardworking men," she replied. And when was she going to see Mac?

After lunch a procession of flowers began to be delivered. There was a huge, beautiful bouquet from the mayor's office and another one from her fellow deputies. She even got one from the Rock Ridge Garden Club, which she didn't know existed. Each time the door to her room creaked open she was hoping she'd see Mac.

Finally, the doctor came in. "How's my patient this afternoon?" Dr. Washburn asked.

"Okay, but I'm curious what's happened to me. I have a lot of pain in my stomach."

Dr. Washburn nodded and then went on to explain about the two stab wounds she'd suffered and the need for him to take out her spleen.

He answered all her questions and she was dismayed to learn she'd be out of commission for about six weeks. "When can I go home?" she finally asked.

"Given no complications, we'll see about kicking you out of here tomorrow afternoon," he replied.

"That would be great." She was already longing to be in her own home and on her sofa.

"I'll check in with you tomorrow and we'll see where we're at."

After the doctor left, Callie found herself napping off and on. All she really wanted now was to see Mac. Did he not intend to check in on her? That thought caused a pain to shoot through her that had nothing to do with a splenectomy.

Dana checked in on her several times and some of the deputies stopped by to see her. And then dinner was served. The evening meal consisted of a thick slice of meatloaf and mashed potatoes all smothered in a dark gravy. There was also corn, a roll and a bowl of mixed fruit.

As she ate, night slowly descended outside the window. When she was finished eating and her tray was taken away, she leaned back against her pillow and turned on the television. Even though she had nothing in particular she wanted to watch, she just needed something to take her mind of Mac.

The night before she'd truly believed she was going to die and she'd mourned over the fact that she thought she'd never see him again. She'd truly believed he had deep feelings for her, so why hadn't he come to check in on her?

Then he was here, standing in the doorway of her room as if she'd conjured him there by sheer thought alone. "Mac," she said softly. She quickly muted the television.

"Hi, Callie." He came into her room and sat in the chair closest to her bed. "I checked in with the doctor several times during the day and he told me you were doing well."

So he did care. He had checked in on her. Her heart lifted and filled her with warmth. "I'm doing okay and I'm hoping to go home tomorrow." She searched his features and saw the lines of exhaustion that radiated out from his eyes. "How are you doing?"

"Better now that I know you're okay and Nathan is in jail. We've spent the day processing his lair. Oh, I brought you something." He reached into his back pocket and withdrew her pink wallet and her key ring.

He set them on the table between them. "Unfortunately, your purse and coat are now in evidence, but I got your wallet and keys because I know what a pain it is to have to get back identification and credit cards and your car and home keys."

"Thank you, that was very thoughtful of you." She wanted him to touch her...to reach out and hold her hand or kiss her forehead. But she could feel a distance from him.

"At some point I need to get a statement from you," he said. "I know you'll need a ride home from the hospital when you're released. How about if I pick you up and take you home and I'll get an official statement then."

"That sounds good," she agreed. She had suffered one of the most traumatic nights of her life and she'd hoped Mac would swoop in today and proclaim his undying love for her. But it was obvious that wasn't going to happen.

He told her about the events of the night before, of finding the old article in the newspaper that had led them to Nathan's house. He explained how they'd confronted Nathan and he'd run. Thankfully they were able to get him under arrest but tragically not before he'd murdered four young women.

They spoke for a few more minutes, the conversation rather stiff and awkward and he finally stood. "I need to get back to the office. I've got tons of paperwork waiting for me there."

"Mac, don't work too late. You have to be exhausted. With Nathan behind bars you can take a moment to breathe." Despite her own physical condition, she worried about him.

He smiled at her, the first real smile since he'd walked into her room. "Thanks, Callie. Call me tomorrow and let me know if you're going to be released and when."

"I will." He started to walk out. "Mac," she said, stopping him in his tracks. He turned around to look at her. There were so many things she wanted to tell him. About loving him…about wanting to spend her life with him… "Never mind," she finally said. "I'll talk to you tomorrow."

A look of relief crossed his handsome features and then with a nod, he was gone.

She pulled her sheet and the thin blanket up closer around her, suddenly cold with the absence of Mac in the room. Nobody would ever make her believe that Mac didn't love her. Even though he'd been distant with her just now, there had been moments when she'd seen that love shining from his eyes.

She had no idea where she stood as a deputy right now, but more importantly she didn't know if Mac was going to open himself up to accepting her love for him and acknowledging his love for her.

Her hope had been to get the killer behind bars by Christmastime and they'd managed to do that. Now her biggest hope was that Mac would tell her how much he loved her and he'd come home to her house for Christmas.

Chapter Fifteen

Callie sat on the edge of the bed waiting for Mac to arrive to take her home. It was just after noon and the doctor had already released her. She plucked at the hospital gown decorated in tiny little blue flowers.

Her clothes had been cut off her the night before, leaving her no choice but to wear the gown home. She also had no coat and no shoes to wear home. Still, she was grateful to leave the hospital behind even though she was still in a fair amount of pain.

Right now, she was just anxious to see Mac again and find out what his mood was with her today. She desperately hoped he was the Mac with soft gray, unguarded eyes and that sexy grin that always tugged at her heart.

"Look who I found coming down the hallway," Dana said as she came into Callie's room pushing a wheelchair in front of her.

Mac followed behind her, a brown blanket

thrown over his shoulder. "Are you ready to get out of here?" he asked Callie.

"Definitely. Is that really necessary?" she asked and pointed to the wheelchair.

"Absolutely," Dana replied. "All our surgery patients get the excitement of riding in our chariot to the exit door. Come on, girlfriend. Have a seat."

Once Callie was in the wheelchair, Dana handed her one of her flower arrangements to carry and Mac draped the blanket around her shoulders. "You're going to need this to go outside in the cold," he said.

As he pulled it closer around her, she caught the familiar scent of him in it and she wanted to keep it wrapped around her forever. "Mac, if you don't mind, could you grab the other flower arrangements while I push her out?"

"No problem," he agreed.

Once they reached the hospital exit door, Mac told Dana and Callie to sit tight while he stowed all the flowers in the back seat of his car. He then left the passenger door of his car open and came back inside.

"Dana, thank you for taking good care of her," Mac said and then leaned down and scooped Callie out of her chair and into his arms. She immediately wrapped her arms around his neck.

Despite her pain and the cold as he stepped out of the door, a rivulet of warmth swept through her. His scent surrounded her and she had to fight the impulse to lean into him.

He lifted her into the car seat and then released her. She pulled the blanket more closely around her as he walked around the car and got into the driver's seat.

"How are you feeling this morning?" he asked once he'd pulled away from the hospital.

"I still have a little pain, both in my wrists and ankles and in my stomach."

"I wanted to kill him," Mac replied and she saw his fingers tighten on his steering wheel. "I so wanted to smash his face in."

"I would have loved to slap him a couple of times myself." She released a deep sigh. "But it's all over now. I survived and you got the killer and the town is safe again."

He shot her that sexy half grin that always half melted her heart. "There's that optimism."

She grinned back at him. "I foresee great days ahead. All I have to do is heal for a little while." She gazed at him for a moment longer. "Will I still have my job when I get better?"

"Of course you will," he replied immediately.

"Uh…which job? Will I be back on the receptionist desk or will I come back as a deputy? I mean, I know I fell for the oldest ruse in the world with Nathan, and that ended up with me being his latest victim, but up until that time I thought I was a good deputy."

"You were a great deputy and I'd love to have you back in that position again. You more than proved yourself and when you're back on your feet, I look forward to swearing you in." He flashed her a quick smile.

"Thank you, Mac. I can't tell you what this means to me," she replied, even though she was hoping for far more from him.

When they got to her house, he asked for her house key and then once again scooped her into his arms. He carried her into the house and gently set her down on the sofa.

"I'll be right back," he said. It took him two trips to get all the flowers in and on her kitchen table. The last thing he did was plug in the lights on her Christmas tree and then he returned to where she'd stretched out on the sofa and sat in the chair facing her.

He pulled out his notebook and set his phone on the coffee table. "Callie, I hate for you to have to revisit everything that has happened to you, but I need to get an official statement from you. Can you do that for me now?"

"I can."

"Do you mind if I record you?"

"Of course not." She watched as he opened the appropriate app on his phone and then her statement began. She started from the time she'd stepped out of her house to go to work and then seeing Nathan seated on the curb.

She had managed to keep all thoughts of Nathan and what she'd endured at his hands out of her mind. But as she went through things with Mac a wealth of emotion began to rise up inside her.

The abject fear she'd endured, the terror of her own impending death and the grief of never seeing Mac again, all of it rose to the surface. When she'd finished telling him everything that had happened, to her horror, she began to weep.

"Ah, Callie, don't cry," he said softly. "Crying is only going to make you hurt more."

"I…ca-can't help it," she said with choked sobs.

She buried her face in her hands as the emotional pain of what she'd been through met the physical pain of her very recent operation. She hurt both inside and out and at the moment she couldn't control her tears.

Then he was on the sofa next to her and pulling her into his arms. She wrapped her arms around him and buried her face in the crook of his neck. He stroked up and down her back and whispered soothing words that slowly began to calm her down. Even after her tears stopped, she remained with her face pressed into the hollow of his throat.

His familiar scent smelled like safety... like love. Her love for him welled up inside her, filling all the spaces in her heart and sweeping away the fear that thoughts of Nathan had created.

"I love you, Mac, I love you so much and if you look deep in your heart, I believe you love me, too." The words tumbled from her, words she hadn't planned on saying in this moment, but she had been unable to keep inside.

He immediately not only sat back from her, but also he stood and moved to the chair once again. "Callie, I told you from the very beginning that I was emotionally unavailable for a relationship." He didn't look at her but rather gazed at some point just over her head.

"Mac, look into my eyes and tell me you aren't in love with me," she said. She wanted this...him...so badly. She wanted a future with Mac. She wanted to have his babies and grow a family with him.

His gaze finally met hers and in the soft gray depths, she believed she saw love. "I am in love with you, Callie," he finally confessed, causing her heart to soar once again. "But that doesn't change anything."

"Why?" she asked in confusion.

He frowned, and raised a hand to knead the back of his neck. His hand dropped back to his side and he released a deep sigh. "When I told you about Amanda leaving me on Christmas Eve, I left out some things."

He got up from his chair, as if unable to sit still as he spoke about his past. "I knew Amanda and I had issues. She hated my job and she wanted a bigger social life than what we had." He began to pace back and forth in front of her sofa. "Two weeks before Christmas Eve, she told me she was pregnant."

Callie looked at him in surprise. Did he have a child with Amanda? Was he afraid Callie wouldn't accept a child of his with another woman? She wouldn't care if he had a dozen kids. She would love them all because they were a part of him.

"When she told me she was pregnant, we promised each other we'd do whatever it took to have a good marriage," he continued. "I cut back on my hours at work and we started going out more."

He paused and drew several deep breaths. "And then came Christmas Eve, when she told me she was leaving me because I wasn't good enough for her, because I bored her and would never be man enough for her. But the real killing blow was she told me she'd had an abortion because I wasn't good enough to be a father to her baby."

His voice broke, letting Callie know just how emotional he was as he told her about this horrid piece of his story. "Oh Mac," she said softly.

He looked at her, his eyes the turbulent gray of storms. "She killed my baby, Callie. She preferred to kill the baby than have me be the father. Doesn't that tell you anything?"

"Yes, it tells me your ex-wife was a selfish, hateful woman and you should be glad to be free of her," Callie replied as she got up from the sofa.

"Well, it tells me that I'm not good enough, I'm not interesting enough to be in a long-term relationship, and in any case I don't ever want to be in a position for a woman to hurt me like that again." He shoved his hands in his pockets as she approached where he stood.

"Oh Mac, she obviously didn't love you the way I love you. I find you fascinating and I know you're a good man…a man who is good enough to be loved." She stood so close to him she could see his individual dark eyelashes, she could almost feel his heartbeat against her own.

"I want you to love me, Mac. I want to marry you and have your babies. I want you to move in here and call this your home. Oh Mac, if you love me even one-tenth as much as I love you, we'll have a happily-ever-after kind of relationship. All you have to do is fully open up your heart." She leaned into him, needing…desperately wanting…him to wrap her in his arms.

Instead, he took a step back from her. Once again his gaze shot just over her head. "I'm sorry, Callie."

"So, you're going to allow a woman's actions from three years ago to stop you from enjoying Christmas…to stop you from ever having a loving relationship again." Emotion clawed up inside her.

He took another step away from her and her heart plummeted to the floor. "Let me know when you're ready to come back to work," he said.

She stared at him. "So, the only difference between you and Nathan is you aren't a killer. But the two of you are just alike in hanging on to a past trauma and not moving past it. I love you, Mac…but I feel sorry for you."

"I'm sorry, Callie," he repeated and then he turned and walked out the front door.

Tears burned at her eyes, tears that began to chase each other down her cheeks. She went back to the sofa and collapsed as deep sobs began to escape her.

She wept for what might have been. She'd truly hoped that by Christmastime, Mac would be home…here with her and ready to build a future together. That's what she'd wanted from Santa, the gift of being together with Mac.

She'd wanted him to hold her while the lights twinkled on the tree and holiday music played. She'd wanted to feed him a Christmas feast over which they could talk about their future plans. She'd wanted to make love to him at night and for him to be the first thing she saw in the mornings.

Now those dreams lay shattered at her feet. However, one of her dreams had come true.

She would return to work as a deputy. But that success felt hollow compared to what she had lost.

She didn't know how long she cried. She finally got up and took one of her pain pills, knowing it would help take away some of her physical pain, but there was nothing she could take, nothing she could do to take away the emotional pain of Mac walking away from her love.

CALLIE SLID THE stuffed turkey into the oven and then closed the door. It was the day before Christmas and she'd decided to do all the cooking for her holiday dinner today for the meal tomorrow.

The house already smelled of cinnamon and apples from the pie she'd baked earlier. She still wanted to make sweet potatoes with brown sugar and cinnamon. On the menu was also a corn casserole with cream cheese, mashed potatoes and gravy, and a cranberry salad.

She'd used her mother's recipes and thoughts of her family flitted through her mind. Physically, she'd felt a little better with each day that had passed. Emotionally she still ached and thoughts of Mac continued to make her cry.

With the cooking all under control, she decided to take a break. She made herself a cup of coffee and then sat at the kitchen table. She stared out the nearby window where the sky was a dark gray that reminded her of Mac's eyes. The forecast was for snow so it was definitely going to be a white Christmas.

Under different circumstances she would have considered it a near-perfect Christmas. There would be snow and good food on the table. She'd survived a serial killer and landed the job she'd wanted to have.

But for it to be perfect Mac would need to be here with her, celebrating their love. She heaved a deep sigh as it began to snow. Mac had called once to see how she was doing and the brief conversation had been incredibly awkward.

Hopefully by the time she returned to work the awkwardness would be gone. He'd be her boss and nothing more. She had about five weeks to stop loving him, but she didn't even know how to begin to do that.

It continued to snow off and on all afternoon. By six o'clock the kitchen had been cleaned, the food was all put away and she had changed into a pair of red pajamas with little snowflakes.

She fixed a fire in the fireplace, made herself a cup of hot chocolate and then stretched out on the sofa to enjoy the sight of her Christmas lights filling the room and the holiday music playing overhead.

The last time she had looked there was about four inches of snow on the ground. Tonight, children everywhere would be waiting for Santa to fly with his magical reindeers to their homes.

Once again tears filled her eyes. She knew she had to get over Mac, but she'd never loved anyone like she did him. She missed him. She missed seeing his handsome face and talking to him about anything and nothing. She missed the sound of his deep laughter and…she could go on and on about the many ways she felt his absence.

The evening slowly wound down. She finished her hot chocolate and thought about going up to bed, but before she could put action to thought, her doorbell rang.

Who would be on her doorstep at this time on a snowy night? Her heart beat an accelerated rhythm as she got up from the sofa. She opened the door to see Mac standing on her doorstep.

Her breath caught in her throat at the same time she steeled herself. He could be here for any number of reasons and she wasn't about to get her hopes up only to have them dashed again.

"Mac," she said as she opened the door to allow him entry.

"Hi, Callie. Do you mind?" He shrugged out of his coat and placed it on the back of the sofa.

"What's up?" she asked as she returned to her spot on the sofa and he sank down on the chair facing her.

Just looking at him broke her heart all over again. "How are you feeling?" he asked.

"Better with each day that passes." She couldn't read him. Surely he hadn't stopped by on a snowy night just to check how she was doing, but there was nothing on his features that gave her a clue as to why he was really here.

"That's good to hear," he replied.

An awkward silence descended. "Mac, it's Christmas Eve and it's snowing like crazy outside," she finally said. "Why are you here?"

He released a deep sigh and looked down at the floor. "I…uh…was wondering if you still feel the same about me."

"You mean am I still in love with you? Oh, Mac, my love for you isn't shallow enough to change in a few days. I'm probably going to love you for the rest of my life."

"I've done a lot of thinking in the last couple of days. I've been so scared about loving you, about believing that we really could have a happy future together." He finally looked up at her, his eyes the soft gray of a dove's wings. "I was so afraid I would never be enough to make you happy, Callie. But what I've realized over these past few days is that my love for you is bigger than my fear."

Hope exploded inside her. Still she remained on the sofa, afraid to fully embrace her hope.

He stood from the chair and approached where she sat. "Callie, I've been such a fool. I'm so in love with you and I can't imagine my future without you in it. I need my Christmas elf. I need the woman who makes me think, who makes me laugh and makes me believe that we can have a forever love."

"Mac." She finally stood and he pulled her right into his arms. When he kissed her, the kiss spoke of passion and dreams and a future filled with love.

Callie's heart expanded as she realized finally her holiday was complete. A serial killer was behind bars. The lights were twinkling on her tree, snow was falling outside her window and her man had really, truly come home for Christmas.

* * * * *

Don't miss other suspenseful titles by
Carla Cassidy:

Stalker in the Shadows
Stalked in the Night
48 Hour Lockdown
Desperate Measures
Desperate Intentions
Desperate Strangers

Available from Harlequin Intrigue!